~ <u>VIRGINS VS ALIENS</u> ~
SEASON 1: "PROM KING"
EPISODE 2 OF 13: "THE VIRGIN LOVE TRIANGLE"

Written by Christi Luv

250K Words (Season 01)
20K Words (Episode 2/13)
87 Pages

Author: Christi Luv
MyTopShelfEditing@Gmail.com

Manager: V. Perkins
(321) 279-7930
HigherPowerPublishing@Gmail.com

TAGLINE

"Fight for love-- with wisdom."

LONG SYNOPSIS

Two secretly chaste celebrity heartthrob best friends fall in love with the same
increasingly neurotic, sexually abstinent, nice girl, posing as her secret admirer on
Valentine's Day, and a wild "Boy Band Rock Star Love Triangle" feud and controversy
erupt into both dangerous and amusing mellow-drama, secret reveals and deadly insanity,
amid the teenishly upstaged backdrop of a strange and creepy alien invasion from outer
space.

SHORT SYNOPSIS

It's Never Been Kissed meets Mars Attacks.
While fighting Mean Girls.

REVIEW/FOREWORD

The substance of "VA" (Season 1) is heartfelt, real and important, but the delivery style is
like a humorous spoof on grossly self-absorbed and over-sexualized teen TV dramas,
albeit giving all the ignored celibate youth and "True Love Waits" lifestylers out there the
glamorous spotlight for once, while parodying trashy pop culture with biting satirical dry
wit.

It's a smart, passionate love story that can make you laugh, cry, gasp, swoon, feel better,
see higher and understand deeper. You won't find a unique adventure like this anywhere
else. The whole 13 episode 1st season may change your life forever ~ and give you
somethin' to talk about for lifetimes to come...

--The Book Club Elite

<u>DEDICATION</u>

For those who love.
For those who wait.
And for those who know that *wisdom*
is what makes you a real man or woman--
not *sex*.

INT. CEKKSEATENE HIGH SCHOOL - BOY'S LOCKER ROOM - SAME

Sammy and Love hear weird creepy clicky clacky breathing noises and look up to see a giant glistening gold alien monster staring at them through creepy fly-like eyes, as it stands across room on other side of lockers, looking like it's going to attack them. They gulp nervously.

                    SAMMY KING
          Wow-- They really upped the budget for senior pranks
          this year. That's a *super* great and authentic looking
          alien monster costume ya got there, guy. What's your
          name?

                    LOVE JONES
               (whispering)
          What are you *doing?*

                    SAMMY KING
               (whispering)
          Trying to befriend the monster to confirm my hope that
          he's human.

                    LOVE JONES
          That does *not* look like a costume and you *know* it,
          Sammy.
               (tittering fearfully)

                    SAMMY KING
          C'mon, get up.

Sammy helps Love up, not taking his eyes off the alien, as he stands in front of her protectively and moves slowly towards school hall exit with her. Suddenly they hear glass crash. They glance at where sound came from, but when they look back across room-- the alien monster is gone.

                    LOVE JONES
          It's gone.

                    SAMMY KING
          Let's go.

They turn to leave but alien monster is suddenly right in front of them, blocking reentry into school halls. They both gasp, startled and back up, as Sammy holds her hand. Sammy turns and quickly hurries Love out of locker room, into gym.

INT. CEKKSEATENE HIGH SCHOOL - GYM - SAME

Sammy runs through empty basketball court with Love, as she holds on to her cupcake
for dear life. He bursts through exit door, into soccer and football field area.

EXT. CEKKSEATENE HIGH SCHOOL - GYM ALLEY WAY - SAME

Sammy and Love look around, bewildered.

                    SAMMY KING
          Where is everybody? And why is it darker than a rainy
          day out here? Cloudy out, but it's still afternoon.

                    LOVE JONES
          There-- in the parking lot!

She points. Sammy and Love run through the school alleyway between the gym and
another building, towards the handful of people they see crowding around, at the front of
the school.

EXT. CEKKSEATENE HIGH SCHOOL - PARKING LOT - SAME

                    SAMMY KING
          HEY! HEY! GUYS! WHAT'S-- WHOA--

Running Sammy stops short, blocking Love with his arm in a protective stance, as he
looks up into the *cloudless* part of the sky, and sees the big black alien spacecraft
hovering over them, above the parking lot. Love gasps as she sees it.

                    SAMMY KING (CONT'D)
          What the--

                    LOVE JONES
          Is that a--

                    SAMMY KING
          --UFO.

                    LOVE JONES
          Piloted by--

                    SAMMY KING
          --Aliens.

                    LOVE JONES
          All the way from--

                    SAMMY KING
--Outer Space.

                    LOVE JONES
Oh my--

                    SAMMY KING
--GOD.

Sammy practically prays it. Puzzled Nick looks away from the UFO that everybody's
staring at when he hears Love's voice, and looks through the crowd until his eyes fall on
her. He smiles. Then he sees Sammy holding her hand. He looks down and away in
troubled thought. Then, unable to handle it, he leaves the crowd and marches through the
parking lot, over to his expensively fancy trendy sports car.

EXT. CEKKSEATENE HIGH SCHOOL - PARKING LOT - CAR - SAME

He pulls out his key remote, unlocks his doors and gets in the driver's seat. He puts the
key in the ignition when--

                    DEVILLE
HIYA NICK!

                    NICK O′ BRIEN
AGH!

Nick drops his keys with a startled jolt and sees cocksure Deville sitting in his backseat,
grinning at him, as his cell phone transforms into a living organism, on the seat next to
him, without anyone noticing.

                    NICK O′ BRIEN (CONT'D)
Holy-- *Deville!* How many times have I told you--
STOP BREAKING INTO MY CAR.

                    DEVILLE
Well if you really want me to *stop* breaking into your
car, then *stop* making me the middle man buyer
whenever you guys wanna buy a new car. It's not *my*
fault I make a copy of every key I ever hand you.

                    NICK O′ BRIEN
That's *literally* the definition of *"my fault"*, Deville.

                    DEVILLE

Oh pish posh. I have a million dollar deal for you guys--
and an EXCELLENT reality TV show vehicle revved
up for Sam, but you're gonna have to talk Sammy into it.

                NICK O' BRIEN
I dunno if you been paying attention to the local Twitter
Instagram Grape-vine of Gossip today, Deville, but me
and Sammy aren't exactly on good-- or ANY-- speaking
terms right now. You'd sooner get him to listen to a
"Twincest Rights Activist" before you'd get him to listen
to me. By the way-- are you seriously still doing your
whole daily *Plot To Take Over The World One Sammy-
King-SexLoveBand-Shady-PR-Trick At A Time* thing
right now, even while we're currently being occupied by
austere extra terrestrials from God-knows-where?

                DEVILLE
             (shrugs apathetically)
Life goes on.

                NICK O' BRIEN
I'm not sure if your ambition *inspires me highly* or
frightens me deeply.
             (notices his face)
Why are the numbers on your face so different from
everybody else's? I haven't noticed much more than
mostly zeros on everybody's right cheek. But yours is
666.

                DEVILLE
I don't ask you about all the zeros on your face or the 1
on your forehead. You don't ask me about all the high
numbers on mine.

                NICK O' BRIEN
Your forehead has a zero on it.

                DEVILLE
Well there. Now we have a number in common. Now
can I rely on you to turn our young strapping Mr. Sex
Candy's head? Or will I have to resort to extreme
measures?

                NICK O' BRIEN
Sex Candy?

                DEVILLE

You know what I mean.

                    NICK O' BRIEN
I am *confident* I do not.

                    DEVILLE
I heard about how you and Sammy are in love with the
same girl, and it looks like she chose him over you.
That's gotta be like having spicy hot pop rocks
exploding up your ass, huh?

                    NICK O' BRIEN
          (irritated)
Whadayou want, Deville? Cause clearly it's more than a
favor.

                    DEVILLE
          (grins wickedly)
I want intel, Nicky-baby--

                    NICK O' BRIEN
          (rolls eyes)
Don't call me that.

                    DEVILLE
I want the scoop, Nicky-boy--

                    NICK O' BRIEN
          (sighs impatiently)
Don't call me that either.

                    DEVILLE
I wanna know-- where you stand, with your bff Sam, so
I know if our little family is divorcing soon-- and which
parent I'll prefer the custody of.

Nick stares at Deville in the rear-view mirror for a beat. Then he looks out the window in
new thought. He looks down, troubled. Sighs darkly. Then he looks back up at Deville.

                    NICK O' BRIEN
Sammy and I are no longer friends, Deville. He's
decided to break up the band and go on his own separate
way. So I'll take over as lead. And I'm down for helping
you get whatever it is you want from him. In my
opinion-- he has it coming to him.

                    DEVILLE

(grins eerily at him)
Perfect. I want you to get him to sign this contract to do
this new reality show called Prom King--

Deville plops 500 page contract in Nick's lap. Nick is stunned by size.

NICK O' BRIEN
Uh-- K-- What's this show about?

DEVILLE
OK so get this, Sammy auditions and dates a bunch of
crazy hot chicks to figure out which one he wants to
give his virginity to on Prom Night. After he wins *Prom
King* title, obvi.

Nick suddenly stares at Deville with alarmed eyes. He notices.

DEVILLE (CONT'D)
Oh, you didn't know? Turns out Sammy left the record
button on after his birthday interview you guys did at
Hot99FM last year. Leanne comes in to seduce him and
he spills all his guts out to her about how he's really
secretly a virgin waiting for love 'n marriage or some
crazy crap like that. Radio station thought it was a
prank, so they sent it to me and asked me if it was a
publicity stunt that I wanted them to air, back when it
happened.

NICK O'BRIEN
You been sittin' on that for half a year? Why? I mean--
you-- *don't* want to air it... *right?*

DEVILLE
Oh no. This is leverage. To get Sammy to do whatever I
want. So of *course* I won't air it--

Nick breathes a sigh of relief.

DEVILLE (CONT'D)
Yet. Prolly tomorrow on Lunch Radio. Then it'll create a
media firestorm here in school, so we can use it as a
diving board to jump into promoting his Prom King
show. Every girl and her milf will be signing up for that
hit reality series once it comes out *at* school that Sammy
King is some secret saint.

NICK O' BRIEN

He's not a saint. None of us are.

                    DEVILLE
I don't care. I just wanna profit off it. You can too now
that you 2 are no longer chummy.

                  NICK O' BRIEN
               (looks down, thinking)
What's the 2nd thesis in your hand?

                    DEVILLE
          (tosses Nick 2nd contract)
This? Oh, right-- I also want you to get him and the
band to sign this contract to play this million dollar
parade at a kid's theme park. It's $1 million for EACH of
you. I need it signed by Prom Night. Preferably sooner.

                  NICK O' BRIEN
             (scans pages of contract)
Wow. That's *awesome*. What parade is it?

                    DEVILLE
Twincest Pride Parade down at Mouse Town Parks. Call
me when it's done.

Cavalier Deville hops out of the car as Nick gawks at the 2nd 500-page contract in his
hands with horrified disgust.

                  NICK O' BRIEN
What the f--

EXT. CEKKSEATENE HIGH SCHOOL - PARKING LOT - SAME

Sammy tugs Love's hand. She looks at him.

                   SAMMY KING
You should call your fam. Make sure they're OK. I gotta
catch up with my aunt and uncle to see if they have any
theological ideas or knowledge on what's happening
here. Since, nobody else seems to know. Or-- just won't
tell us. I want you to meet my mom too, but she's still
overseas at another rocket science convention with my
stepdad 'n stepbrother. I talk about you with my aunt 'n
uncle when ever I see them. I'd like you to meet them.

                   LOVE JONES

                    (heart-warmed)
          Aww, Sammy-- You're so sweet. Sure. When?

                    SAMMY KING
          Now.

                    LOVE JONES
          Oh. OK. Let's go then.

She shrugs. He smiles and guides the back of her waist with his hand as he escorts her
away from crowd. REPORTER KATHY, 30s, gets excited when she finally sees Sammy,
like she's been waiting for him all day long. She smacks her camera guy's arm, pastes on
a big TV smile and rushes over, as Sammy walks Love toward the parked cars.

                    REPORTER KATHY
          Sammy! Any comment on the viral video that just *broke
          the internet* today, showing an *explosive* fight between
          you 'n your *best* friend and SexLove bandmate, *Nick
          O'Brien?*

                    SAMMY KING
          No comment.

                    REPORTER KATHY
          What about the rumors that you and he love the same
          girl? Who you're holding hands with right now-- your
          classmate *Love Jones?*

                    SAMMY KING
          No comment.

                    REPORTER KATHY
                    (flustered, desperate*)*
          Wha-- Well-- *What about the aliens?*

                    SAMMY KING
                    (stops, turns)
          I think we should *nuke* all these *stupid* Valentine Aliens
          outta the *sky* until they *disappear* and take all their
          stupid face numbers *with them.*

                    REPORTER KATHY
                    (gasps gratefully)
          Thank you Sammy! We appreciate it!

                    SAMMY KING
          No problem Kathy.

Fame-fatigued Sammy nods tiresomely and resumes walking away with Love. Then he sighs knowingly to himself and speaks up, in a dull, over-it voice without stopping or turning around.

                    SAMMY KING (CONT'D)
          HOW ARE THE KIDS?

                    REPORTER KATHY
               (shouts excitedly)
          GOOD, GOOD! MATTY JUST TURNED 4!

                    SAMMY KING
               (throws up air salute)
          TELL HIM I SAID HAPPY BIRTHDAY.

                    REPORTER KATHY
          I WILL!

She waves blissfully at Sammy even though he's still walking away with his back to her, unable to see her. Love looks back curiously to see Kathy gesture goofy *SCORE* with her arm like she just made a big soccer goal, as Sammy takes Love to his expensively spacious and fancy-sophisticated luxury car. Nobody notices cameraman's camera transform into a living organism as it sits casually on his shoulder.

Meanwhile, Nick runs up to the crowd and wades through it til he reaches the people who were standing in front of Sammy and Love.

                    NICK O' BRIEN
          Hey-- you know where Sammy went?

People shake their heads or shrug and go back to staring up at the spacecraft. Nick huffs-- frustrated-- grabs his phone and texts on it.

EXT. CEKKSEATENE HIGH SCHOOL - PARKING LOT - CAR - SAME

Sammy unlocks his car as Love surveys it.

                    LOVE JONES
          Wow. Nice car.

                    SAMMY KING
          All the time I been drivin' this whip to school 'n you *jus*
          now noticin' it?

He sucks teeth playfully with a charming smile as he opens her door for her like a gentleman. She giggles and gets in. Then he goes back around to his driver's side and gets in.

                    LOVE JONES
          I'm not really a car person. I tend to only notice pink
          cars, cupcake cars, and cars that I'm actually getting
          inside of. Oh-- and crashed cars. Then again, I might be
          more focused on the people in the crash than I am on
          what type of cars they crashed...

Sammy chuckles as he checks his beeping cell phone and reads Nick's message: *"Jus
found out Deville will sabotage / out u 2moro @ lunch. Stay home. DONT SIGN
ANYTHING."* Sammy smirks.

                    SAMMY KING (V.O.)
          Yeah right. Jus so I give you the whole day to try and
          steal my Love away from me again? You mus be out yo
          ever-lovin' mind, boi.

Sammy starts the car and smiles at giddy Love.

                    SAMMY KING
          Vroom vroom?

                    LOVE JONES
          Vroom vroom!

EXT. CHURCH - YOUTH CENTER - PARKING LOT - SAME DAY

Sammy parks car, turns the engine off and takes Love's hand.

                    SAMMY KING
          Aright now, Love-- the youth center people are fairly
          young, but some people at my church are very old, and
          don't get enough TV, web or FM radio to know anything
          about my life or-- my career. They jus think of me as
          that sweet kid Sammy King who they heard grew up to
          be a movie star.
                    (sighs knowingly)
          I'd like to keep it that way, and do everything possible to
          keep any gossip about us out of their mouths.

Love just stares at him blankly for a moment.

                    LOVE JONES
          OK, you do realize this is a *church*, right? All church
          people *do* is *gossip*. Especially if they're *jealous* or
          petty. Then they just straight up lock you out of *talking*
          or even sharing your *talents* with them.

                         SAMMY KING
          Wow. *You* have some unexpected church *baggage*, Miss
          Church Girl.

                         LOVE JONES
          You have no idea.

Sammy laughs as he gets out of his car, closes the door, goes around, opens her car door,
and offers her a hand up. She takes it.

                         LOVE JONES (CONT'D)
          What a gentleman, Mr. Sammy King. How long will
          this chivalry last?

                         SAMMY KING
          Prolly til we have our 1st fight.

She scoffs, laughingly surprised and playfully nudges him. He laughs honestly,
pretending he misspoke as he shuts the door.

                         SAMMY KING (CONT'D)
          Oops, I meant-- it'll *never* end, beautiful. *Everyone*
          knows that *chivalry--* is *FOREVER*.

She smirks, shaking her head, as he laughs at the state of their culture. Then he folds his
arm up and nudges her with his elbow.

                         SAMMY KING (CONT'D)
              M'lady.

She looks, realizing he's urging her to lock her arm in his. She smiles warmly at this and
wraps her arm around his. He smiles proudly at her, and they walk up grassy knoll
together, toward youth center lobby. Behind them, Sammy's car radio transforms into a
living organism.

INT. CHURCH - YOUTH CENTER - LOBBY - SAME

Sammy opens the glass door for Love and they walk in together. RECEPTIONIST
CYNTHIA MAGDALENE, 19, sits at desk, laughing on phone. She glances up to greet
them and gasps, stunned, wide eyed.

                         RECEPTIONIST CYNTHIA MAGDALENE
              Sammy!

                         SAMMY KING
                   (stunned, unsure)
              Cynthia--

SAMMY KING (V.O.)
Cynthia Magdalene? Oh no. Why is she here?

SAMMY KING
I-- I thought you quit this job to go work at a call center.
(fake polite chuckle)

SAMMY KING (V.O.)
Not come back just to scare my new girlfriend away...

RECEPTIONIST CYNTHIA MAGDALENE
Yeah, they fired me for talking to people too much, so I
came back home.

SAMMY KING (V.O.)
And you couldn't find *another* home?

SAMMY KING
Oh-- Well-- *welcome back home.*

RECEPTIONIST CYNTHIA MAGDALENE
Thanks. Welcome back to *you* too.

SAMMY KING
Thanks, thanks.

Love looks between them awkwardly, like she can tell there's history between them but
she can't quite figure it out. Love sees that Cynthia has a #1 on her forehead, #101 on her
chin, #69 on her nose, #0 on her right cheek and #3 on her left. Cynthia smiles
flirtatiously at Sam, as her desktop PC discretely transforms into a living organism.

RECEPTIONIST CYNTHIA MAGDALENE
Still looking *dashing* as *always*.

SAMMY KING
(blushing nervously)
Thank you, thank you. You too. Uh-- this is Love Jones.
My classmate and-- my-- *girlfriend*-- now.

Cynthia's face drops as she looks Love up and down, before abruptly pasting on a clearly
fake smile of pretend joy.

RECEPTIONIST CYNTHIA MAGDALENE
Oh *wow. You* must be the girl who broke up Nick and
Sammy's *legendary* friendship. *Aww*, you're so *pretty!*
No *wonder* they gave up all of their band's mega fame,
fortune and fans *just* for *you!* Hi, how *are* you?

SAMMY KING (V.O.)
And it begins...

She puts her hand out for a handshake, still fake-grinning. Not the least bit clueless to her
back-handed compliment, Love shoots Sammy an irritated, knowing look that he takes in
with a knowing nod, as he looks down a bit somberly. Then she looks back at Cynthia,
plasters on her own fake smile, and shakes her hand graciously, nodding at her.

LOVE JONES
Well, you know what the good Lord says about true
love-- it's unconditional. I mean, Sammy giving up his
fame, fortune and fans for me in 1 little schoolyard fight
is still no comparison to getting beat down. Dragged
through the mud. Viciously slandered. Nailed to a cross
by your hands and feet. And then left for dead like a
wounded animal for umteen grueling hours on end.
With no drop of water in sight. Trapped between 2 low-
life crooks. At the single age of 33. After doing nothing
but giving your all to everyone. Turning water into
wine. Multiplying all those fishies and loaves. Healing
the sick 'n cripple. Making the blind see. And even
teaching people how to walk on water. And then being
betrayed by the very human race you came down to save
in total self-sacrifice. Dying for the same people who do
nothing but waste their lives trash-talkin' you. Startin'
mess. Gettin' wasted. Lovelessly screwin' anybody out
of wedlock. Hurtin' innocent people routinely.
Worshiping sex, fame, power and gold, never valuing
their souls or anybody else's. And destroying the
historical empire of faith, hope, love, peace and
salvation that you worked-- and died-- so hard to build.
Like the very concept of The Holy Bible is completely
lost on them--
(titters politely, then is serious-
faced again)
But yes. True love is unconditional. And I'm blessed to
have met a young man of God who knows how to love
me the way Jesus loves the church. A man who values
my heart and soul over power, fame and gold.
(smiles knowingly)
I need the ladies room. Where may that be?

SAMMY KING (V.O.)
Wow--

Sammy admires Love. Speechless Cynthia points to the restrooms with a funny look of both God-smacked guilt and confused contempt. Love nods at Sammy, who wants to laugh, and she prances off.

INT. CHURCH - YOUTH CENTER - LOBBY - BATHROOM - SAME

Love enters bathroom, rests her hands on the sink and eyes herself in the mirror with an impatient huff, clearly not enjoying being here-- or catching hell from Sammy's fans. Then she gasps and touches the 5 numbers on her face, just now seeing them. Every number's #0 except for her forehead, which says #2. Alien tentacles quietly ooze out of a toilet in the stall behind her as she looks down at the running water, rinsing her face and hands. She picks up her cupcake and considers eating it with a dubious stare, not seeing tentacles rise behind her.

INT. CHURCH - YOUTH CENTER - LOBBY - SAME

Out in lobby, Sammy just smiles politely at Cynthia, as she watches him like a hawk, admiring him up and down, while absentmindedly chewing on the back of a pen.

                    SAMMY KING
          I'm not-- quitting the band. Jus-- FYI.

He shrugs whateverishly. She just nods at him with an oddly knowing stare. Sammy sort of looks away in awkward silence.

INT. CHURCH - YOUTH CENTER - LOBBY - BATHROOM - SAME

Love starts unwrapping her cupcake to eat it. Then she stops, sighs, shakes her head at herself, wraps it back up, turns sharply-- and exits the bathroom, right as the tentacles lunge out and barely miss her.

INT. CHURCH - YOUTH CENTER - LOBBY - SAME

Love returns to silent lobby and smiles cheerfully at Sammy.

                    SAMMY KING
          Ready?

She nods cheerfully. He gives her his arm again. She takes it, and he nods a cordial goodbye to Cynthia as he walks with Love toward the hallway of offices. Cynthia watches them curiously, before quickly grabbing her phone and texting up a storm.

INT. CHURCH - YOUTH CENTER - OFFICE HALLWAY - SAME

Sammy and Love saunter down the hall.

                    SAMMY KING
You handled that well, m'lady. With the poise of a
gracious queen. Worried for a sec. That girl usually gets
under people's skin.

                    LOVE JONES
Of course she got under my skin, Sammy. She *hates* me.
Who is she? You *clearly* have *history* with her.

                    SAMMY KING
It's a long story.

                    LOVE JONES
I've got time.

                    SAMMY KING
          (sighs, conceding)
Aright. That was Cynthia Magdalene. She and I-- We
sorta... *kiddishly* dated back in Junior High. Before I
found you. I thought she was a nice girl.
          (realizes, shrugs)
She *was* a nice girl. Until *I* became her boyfriend. Then
she got popular really fast, hangin' out with some of my
fast show biz friends, pickin' up their demons 'n bad
habits, listenin' to my crazy manager Deville. And
suddenly she started becoming this fast-tail, hard-living,
super snotty mean girl who wanted to live fast, die
young, drink up, smoke out 'n screw the world, before
even hitting high school. Then I saw you and I broke it
off with her. But by then she'd developed a drinking
problem 'n I heard she even went into rehab. So I sent
her a gift basket and polite correspondence while she
was in there, to show my support. But she took it wrong
and started telling everyone we were getting married or
some craziness I never even suggested *playfully*. Then
she got out and I heard she was doing well but still
antagonizing people, flaunting her latest sports cars or
diamond rings, and talking about me like I was her
future husband. So I kinda stopped coming here after
school, jus to avoid her. Cause she was always here.
Then I heard she quit here to get a higher paying gig
somewhere else. So I came back here. After school. And
today I see, she's back. Of course she's back. Cause I
brought you here for the 1st time today. So it's Murphy's
Law that she has to be back today.

He shakes his head as he stops at an office door. Love chuckles in surprised appreciation for his candor.

                    LOVE JONES
        Wow-- That really *was* a long story.

                    SAMMY KING
        I *told* you.

He chuckles with her, opening the door for her. She stops, before entering, and looks at him in sudden realization.

                    LOVE JONES
        So *that's* part of why you waited 4 years to reveal
        yourself to me. You were afraid I'd be like *Cynthia* and
        totally unravel, because I wasn't prepared for your crazy
        life.

                    SAMMY KING
                (realizes, thinking)
        Wow. I never really thought about it, but-- yeah, maybe.
        Guess I was afraid I'd be a bad influence on *your* life
        too. But, in all fairness, I also enjoyed just having a
        connection with someone who didn't know who I was.

                    LOVE JONES
                (smiles fondly)
        I always knew who you were, Sammy King-- Deep *deep*
        down-- On the inside.

He smiles warmly at her, kisses her cheek and follows her into the office. Tentacles slime by, inside of an air vent behind Sammy.

INT. CHURCH - YOUTH CENTER - UNCLE ROMEO'S OFFICE - SAME

Sammy and Love are greeted with the soft hum of snoring as they silently enter the quiet office. Sammy looks over at the desk and sees that it's empty. He looks over at the couch and sees his uncle stretched out on it, taking a power nap, with his signature red WWJD? Christ cap lightly covering his eyes.

                    LOVE JONES
        Oh he's sleeping--

Love whispers, but a now-grinning Sammy lightly sshes her, with his index finger to his mouth, and stealthily tip-toes across the room, leading her into the bathroom with him.

                    LOVE JONES (CONT'D)

What are we doing?

She whispers as he almost closes the door, pulls out his cell phone, opens an app and
dials a number, with a laugh in his voice.

                         SAMMY KING
              Watch--

Suddenly a ringing sound echoes from the desktop on Uncle Romeo's desk via a Skype-
like program. After 5 rings it self-answers and a live video of Sammy and Love pops up
on the screen, as Uncle Romeo murmurs groggily in increasingly awakening sleep.
Sammy represses laughter as he switches up his sound and shouts into his phone with a
high-pitched silly voice, mocking loud, distressed teenage girl.

                    SAMMY KING (CONT'D)
              UNCLE ROMEO!!!

                        UNCLE ROMEO
              MEH!!!

Uncle Romeo jumps up, tired and bewildered, wiping his face.

                         SAMMY KING
                    (whiny valley voice)
              *OH MY GOD! UNCLE ROMEO! HE, LIKE, TOTALLY
              GOT ME PREGNANT AND NOW I DON'T KNOW
              WHAT TO DO!! SHOULD I ABORT THE BABY NOW
              OR KEEP IT??*

Groggy Uncle sighs, clears throat and gets up, stretching.

                        UNCLE ROMEO
              No no-- don't abort. Keep him. Or her. We'll help you.
              Where are you?

                         SAMMY KING
              *OH MY GOD I'M RIGHT HERE! IN YOUR
              COMPUTER! DUH!*

Love gets it now and starts giggling with Sammy, both of them in hushed chuckles. Uncle
Romeo looks confused as he looks around and over at his desk, and goes over to it.

                        UNCLE ROMEO
              No I mean where are you *located* now, miss--

Uncle Romeo sits at desk as Sammy faces the camera of his phone toward the floor. His
uncle searches computer screen for an image.

UNCLE ROMEO (CONT'D)
Where-- did you go?

SAMMY KING
*OH MY GOD I THINK THE BABY'S COMING OUT
NOW!!!*

UNCLE ROMEO
(confused)
What? OK, stay calm. Tell me where you are. I'll call
911 and send help over to you now--

SAMMY KING
*NOOO! I THINK IT'S AN **ALIEN** BABY!!*

UNCLE ROMEO
(bewildered, realizes)
OK, you're pranking me. Who is this?

SAMMY KING
(laughing with Love)
AREN'T YOU GONNA COME SAVE ME???

UNCLE ROMEO
(sighs, yawning)
I'm goin' back to my nap now.

BAM! Sammy abruptly SLAMS the bathroom door open and JUMPS out in front of
Uncle Romeo, making him jump with a start.

SAMMY KING
BUT WE JUST GOT HERE!

UNCLE ROMEO
Cheeze-its, Sammy! You almost gave me a heart attack!

Sammy cracks up laughing as Uncle Romeo shakes his head with a kiddish chuckle, half-
relieved and half-humored. Sammy steps over to give him some dap and a hug. Love
follows him, still giggling.

SAMMY KING
You should really lock your door when you nap, Unc.
Ya never know who could jus *pop* up and *surprise* you.

UNCLE ROMEO

Apparently. There's a space alien invasion brewing up
above us, and yet my biggest surprise here today was
you. --*Who's this?*

He looks at Love, who smiles and waves. Sammy stands regally and beams proudly as his
Uncle grabs a swig of bottled water.

                          SAMMY KING
        This-- is *Love Jones.*

Uncle almost chokes on his water. Looks between them, seriously.

                          UNCLE ROMEO
        THE-- Love Jones?

                          SAMMY KING
                    (nods merrily)
        THE-- Love Jones-- Yep!

                          LOVE JONES
                    (chuckles bashfully)
        THE-- Love Jones? Wow! Yall are makin' me feel
        famous haha!

                          UNCLE ROMEO
        You are, Miss Love. In this family, *you*-- are definitely
        famous. Nice to finally meet you, Love. You're
        everything he said you were.

He extends his hand out to her with a wowed but worried smile, and Love shakes it
cheerfully, not quite catching his curious concern.

                          LOVE JONES
        Thank you! You too!

She chuckles and Sammy grins at her both proudly and fondly, as Uncle Romeo's eyes
gaze upon the number on her forehead.

                          UNCLE ROMEO
        Number 2. No wonder you boys got into a fight today.

Uncle Romeo glances at Sammy, then looks down, pondering it, as Sammy tilts his head
at him with a furrowed brow.

                          SAMMY KING
        What-- You heard about that? During your-- Power
        Nap?

UNCLE ROMEO
I only got 5 minutes. Before that I got a text from
somebody showing a viral clip of you and Nick beating
the *crap* out of each other.

SAMMY KING
(smirks)
You mean of ME beating the crap out of HIM.

UNCLE ROMEO
No, you mighta won the fight-- but you both got
damaged by it.

SAMMY KING
(irked, changes topic)
What's it got to do with the numbers on Love's face?
Did you and Aunt Jules figure it out yet? Where is she,
by the way?

UNCLE ROMEO
She's over in The Fellowship Hall, overseeing all the
charity meal giveaways in the Community Food Pantry.
It's Free Food Day. So everybody's over there for a
while. She'll be over soon, to have lunch with me, when
she gets a break. So she can meet the beautiful love of
your life, Future Wifey here.

He leans back in his chair, as he throws a relaxed smile at them both. Love smiles.
Sammy nods with a cordial smile, still a bit concerned.

SAMMY KING
So ya figured out the numbers meaning?

UNCLE ROMEO
We have a working theory.

Romeo nods lightly. Sammy and Love trade anxious glances.

SAMMY KING
So what do all the numbers mean?

Uncle Romeo heaves a tired sigh as he glances down and cracks his neck in grimacing
thought. As if he's unsure how to say it. He doesn't notice the office phone on his desk as
it begins to transform into a slowly moving, breathing living organism.

UNCLE ROMEO

The numbers on our faces appear to be... the
metaphysical diagnostic evidence-- of our behavioral
truth... in the realm of-- sex, love and relationships.

                    SAMMY KING
               (stares blankly)
Come again?

                    UNCLE ROMEO
Your Aunt Jules and I have the unfortunate honor of
being privy to all the goings on in our church youths'
lives. For some reason they trust us, and-- they tell us
everything.
               (sighs to himself)
I really wish they wouldn't.
               (shakes head grimly)
Any way-- Knowing it all, we saw a pattern. Both
between them and between your aunt and me, whose 5
face numbers are identical.

Curiously, Love registers the #1 on his chin, #1 on his forehead, and #0s on his nose and
cheeks.

                    UNCLE ROMEO (CONT'D)
Jus like us, it correlated numbers on their faces, with
their romantic love or sexual behavior-- or lack thereof.
For example, the number on your chin is how many
people you've had natural consensual sex with. The
number on your nose is how many people you've had
unnatural consensual sex with.

                    SAMMY KING
               (understanding)
Sodomy.

                    UNCLE ROMEO
               (nodding)
Correct.

He goes silent. Sammy looks between him and Love anxiously.

                    SAMMY KING
And the number on our foreheads?

                    UNCLE ROMEO
               (sighs knowingly)

The number on your foreheads-- represents-- how many
people-- you've ever actually... *loved... Romantically.*

Something in Sammy's gut appears to sink as he slowly gazes back over at Love, and
focuses on the #2 on her forehead.

SAMMY KING
Two... You really *are* in love with *both* of us.

Love's heart beats fast. She looks down sheepishly, trying to process, as if suddenly the
#1 on his forehead, amid all zeros, means so much more now-- and she feels guilty for
something she had no control over.

UNCLE ROMEO
Relax, Sammy. It's OK. Just because she loves you *both*
doesn't mean she doesn't love you *enough*-- or love you
even *more*. She's here with *you,* isn't she? So *you* won.
It's not her fault Nick didn't tell either of you that he was
in love with her, back when you both started pursuing
her in secret.

SAMMY KING
(nods, then looks at him)
I-- didn't-- tell you that. We haven't told anybody that.
So how'd you--
(thunderstruck)
You knew? Uncle Rome-- You *knew* ALL this time
Nick was after her while *I* was, and you didn't *tell* me?
How could you be so unfair?

UNCLE ROMEO
(chuckles knowingly)
Unfair? Sammy, it wasn't my place to betray Nick's
confessional confidence, or to ruin your lifelong
friendship, or to speed up your reveal with Love, just so
the 2 of you boys could fight, crash 'n burn whatever
either of you had with her to the ground, before you
even made it to prom night. And if you wanna be *fair*
about it-- Nick *saw* her first, Nick *talked* to her first, and
Nick fell in *love* with her first, so Nick's *entirely* entitled
to feel the way he feels. And considering that she now
loves *both* of you, you should have enough respect for
both *his* feelings and *hers* to sit them both down and
have a rational, honest conversation about it. He's your
lifelong best friend, Sammy. You 2 have been brothers
since ya were 2.

SAMMY KING

4.

UNCLE ROMEO
WHATEVER. Be wise and realize that you have a few
things to consider here, Sammy. And I'm not even
talkin' about the superficial ones, like foolishly blowin'
up your band or career over a forgivable spat with your
top boy. I'm talkin' the deep and intangible stuff that you
can't buy or replace. Like 1-- Ya need to face the fact
that you're never gonna find another best friend like
Nick. You have too much shared foundational history,
camaraderie chemistry, and ride-or-die-hard loyal
brotherly bond-- which no other "bro you know" is
EVER gonna top. 2-- You're rich and famous now,
Sammy-- which means everyone you meet might have
an agenda. And the only people you know for sure that
you can really *trust* are friends like Nick. Who-- for
better or worse-- has ALWAYS had your back. And 3--
LOVE IS NOT A HOCKEY PUCK, SAMMY. And I
mean both the girl and the feeling. Ya can't jus smack
love into your hockey net, say love is yours, 'n call it a
day of victory. It's not that simple. And *definitely* not
that *easy*. *Your* feelings for Love are real. *Nick's* feelings
for Love are real. And *Love's* feelings for *both* of you
are real. You need to be enough of a friend to BOTH of
them to address it-- openly and cautiously-- with fair
regard for *both* of them-- and *their* inner conflicts-- not
just *your* passion and pride.

Silence swallows the room. Love clears her throat nervously.

LOVE JONES
I jus-- have to-- go visit the little girl's room right quick.
Heheh...

A suddenly shy Love coos an anxiously breathy little laugh as she glances uncomfortably
between the 2 of them, with a slight nod. She leaves her cupcake on the desk and quickly
bows out of the room, fleeing the scene as she exits back out into the hallway. Sammy
stares daggers of both youthful hurt and righteous anger at his uncle.

SAMMY KING (V.O.)
Why is EVERYTHING I planned today blowing up in my
face?

SAMMY KING

I respect your wisdom, Uncle Rome-- but you didn't
have to say all that in front of Love.

                    UNCLE ROMEO
Yes I did. Cause she needed to hear it just as much as
you did-- and it mighta taken you another 4 years to
truly acknowledge it. And by then she might've either
resented you or grown tired of the emotional prison of
your relational dominance over her, so much so that you
lose her to Nick regardless. Look-- I don't know who
she loves more-- or *if* she even loves one of you more. I
just know psychology. It's not the useless college degree
my father said it was. It really helps my ministry, my
relationships *and* my advice. And all I'm trying to do--
is save you from clumsily losing the love of your life by
default. I know how much she means to you. How much
she means to *both* of you. And I'd love to play
Switzerland 'n not have a horse in this race, but I know
by judging from what you 2 guys have told me, that she
brings out the righteous *man* in you Sammy, and the
desperate *child* in Nick. So I am rooting for you,
Sammy, I really am. But if you steamroll your way
through this, you're gonna lose her to him eventually--
and if that happens, I'd feel better believing it was
because it was meant to be, not because you jus
needlessly shot yourself in the foot without knowing it.

                    SAMMY KING
                 (nods, thinking about it)
You know he kissed her right after I kissed her first,
right?

                    UNCLE ROMEO
Sammy-- I'm not saying that all of his actions are right.
I'm just saying that his *feelings* MATTER. And so do
hers. And you need to show them that you know that.
That's all.

                    SAMMY KING
                 (sighs in thought)
Aright. How do I do that?

INT. CHURCH - YOUTH CENTER - OFFICE HALLWAY - SAME

Love exits Uncle Romeo's office, turns and bumps into Nick.

                        LOVE JONES
Oh! Sorry--

                        NICK O′ BRIEN
Sorry--

                        LOVE JONES
Nick!

                        NICK O′ BRIEN
Love...

She looks almost petrified by the surprise. He looks stunned and uncertain, but still
interested to see her, albeit with a now suddenly neutered excitement. Neither of them
notice any of the alien tentacles quietly sliming by, inside the air vents above them.

                        LOVE JONES
              You-- maybe shouldn't go in there.

                        NICK O′ BRIEN
Sammy's in there?

                        LOVE JONES
Yeah.

                        NICK O′ BRIEN
                    (nods, cutting eyes)
They gonna be a while?

                        LOVE JONES
                       (nodding)
Probably.

                        NICK O′ BRIEN
                    (nods, looks down)
Hey, uh... Can we-- *talk?*

                        LOVE JONES
Sure. What's up?

                        NICK O′ BRIEN
                 (nods toward end of hall)
I mean in private.

                        LOVE JONES
                 (nervously shrugging)
We are in private, Nick.

NICK O' BRIEN
(sighs knowingly)
Where no one can eavesdrop on us or interrupt us at the
wrong moment.

LOVE JONES
(gulps anxiously)
I don't think that's a very good idea... Last time we
talked, it-- kind of escalated into an --unexpected burst
of lustful passion, that morphed into an epic viral video
beatdown battle between you and your commanding
best friend. Who I am officially seeing now.

NICK O' BRIEN
(looks down, saddened)
So you don't really love me. OK--
(nods to self)
I'll try to keep you two's *wedding* out of my *suicide*
letter then.

Nick huffs off away from her, down the hall, and turns the corner. Love inwardly gasps in
stunned, wide eyed shock, abandoning uncertainty.

LOVE JONES
Suicide??

She quickly turns around and scurries down the hall, after him.

LOVE JONES (CONT'D)
Nick! Wait!

She turns corner and stops short, realizing he's not there. She checks every door, as an
alien tentacle oozes out of a vent and stalks her all the way down the hall, about to
pounce on her, when suddenly-- the last door opens and Love saunters in, once again just
missing the lunge of an alien tentacle that whips at her back, as door closes behind her.

INT. CHURCH - YOUTH CENTER - BRIDAL ROOM - SAME

Love enters, shutting the door in the half-lit room, and sees Nick sitting on the couch,
leaned over, face down and elbows to knees, with his hands laced together over his head.
Tentatively, Love walks over, sits, and puts a gentle hand on his back.

LOVE JONES
Nick. What-- are you talking about? You-- You weren't-
- *serious. Right?*

                          NICK O′ BRIEN
What's it matter? You don't care. You just do whatever
Sammy says like a doll he controls.

                          LOVE JONES
                      (curiously defensive)
He does *not* control me.

                          NICK O′ BRIEN
Coulda fooled me.

                          LOVE JONES
Well he revealed himself to me 1st and he kissed me 1st.
I owe him 1st loyalty for that.

                          NICK O′ BRIEN
What about loyalty to me? *I* found you 1st. *I* loved you
1st. Am *I* that *worthless* to you?

                          LOVE JONES
                     (gasps, shaking head)
Oh no, no, oh my gosh, no, Nick--

                          NICK O′ BRIEN
                    (head-nod, bitter smirk)
Doesn't matter. My step-dad's been right about me all
these years. I'm not good enough, not strong enough, not
man enough. I'm a worthless piece of crap. I destroyed
my friendship with Sammy. I lost my relationship with
you. Now all I am is in the way. I don't deserve to live. I
might as well just die.

He looks away-- dramatically. She shakes head-- mortified.

                          LOVE JONES
Oh my God, Nick, no, stop! What are you saying?? You
can't possibly *believe* that! Your step-dad is *nuts*. Stop
listening to him!

                          NICK O′ BRIEN
It's true. It's true. I'm nothing.

Love sees tears well up in Nick's eyes and cascade down his face as he shakes his head,
repeating his words over and over. Desperate to stop this serious downward spiral, Love
quickly hugs Nick, shushing him, and holding him in a tight embrace, as he sniffs back

tears, and tears well up in her eyes too. But he keeps repeating his negative self-degrading, until she just gives up and kisses him. Suddenly he goes silent, as he kisses her back. She stops to look at him with crying eyes.

LOVE JONES

You are *not* worthless.

Nick smiles meekly at her with The Puppy Pout, and the involuntary *slight* glimmer of a grin that's way too giddy and self-assured for someone who's seriously hopeless.

NICK O' BRIEN

But I *feel* worthless. Friendless. Loveless.

He starts spiraling again. She kisses him again. He kisses her and slyly slips his hand beneath her school shirt, cupping the small of her back in the palm of his hand, pulling her into him as he kisses her sensually. She realizes her renewed predicament and pulls away from him a bit.

LOVE JONES

Sammy--

NICK O' BRIEN

--is not in the room with us right now-- so let's leave it
that way.

He kisses her passionately, takes off his shirt, revealing *his* impressive muscles, to reel her back in. She inadvertently grins gleefully at his masculine form as he leans her back against the couch, repositioning himself atop her. As they kiss, fluorescent lights on the ceiling above them begin to transform into moving, breathing, living organisms.

INT. CHURCH - YOUTH CENTER - UNCLE ROMEO'S OFFICE - SAME

Sammy and Uncle Romeo continue to hash it out at his desk, as the screen on the newly living organism landline phone starts speeding through the phone's data on its digital screen without them seeing it.

UNCLE ROMEO

Well, for starters-- ya need to let her go.

SAMMY KING

(horrified)

What?

SAMMY KING (V.O.)

(horrified)

What?

                    UNCLE ROMEO

If she kissed you *both*, then I think she's *confused*,
Sammy. So now's not the time to lock her down and
make her choose you out of *cerebral obligation.* Now's
the time to let her figure out which one of you she feels
most at home with-- *on her own*-- so she can choose you
out of heartfelt *LOVE,* Sammy. You've had a *million*
girls to choose from before you decided to finally reveal
yourself to Love. So has Nick.

                    SAMMY KING (V.O.)
                        (smirks)
Yeah, not good, honest, *quality* girls.

                    UNCLE ROMEO

But what's Love had to choose from? Two secret
admirers she thought were the same *ONE* guy. So now
it's *her* turn to "see what's out there"-- *only between the
2 of you*-- and finally decide-- of her own accord-- who
she'd rather take a leap of faith with.

                    SAMMY KING (V.O.)

Wait-- *What's he saying?*

                    SAMMY KING
                        (disgusted)
Pastor Romeo-- Are you saying that I need to encourage
the *love of my life* to go *"sew her oats"* with my *best
friend,* before she *finally* decides to *settle down* with
me? *Or* him?

                    UNCLE ROMEO
                        (taken aback)
What? No. That's not what I said. Is that how it
sounded?

                    SAMMY KING

That's how it sounded.

                    UNCLE ROMEO

That's not what I meant.

                    SAMMY KING

Then what did you mean?

                    UNCLE ROMEO

I meant that you just need to give her a moment to *drift*,
Sammy. Give her some space to breathe and just let her
get to know you both in person. See who you both really
are face-to-face, so she can figure out which one of you
she feels the strongest for, and the most comfortable
with, for the long-haul. She has to choose you because
you're the one she *loves* more. Not because you're the
one who *kissed* her first. And you need to let her drift
just to cut the giant Forbidden Fruit Fever out of the
equation all together.

> SAMMY KING
> (confused)
> *Forbidden Fruit Fever?* Whaya mean?

> UNCLE ROMEO
> I mean, if you stop making Nick look like the off-limits
> *bad boy* in your lil love triangle dynamic, she'll stop
> feeding into it with his *stolen kisses in the night* shtick,
> and she'll start to see Nick more clearly. Which is good
> for you, because if she sees you both more clearly, she's
> much more likely to pick you.

> SAMMY KING

Why?

Sammy grimaces as Romeo's desk phone abruptly stops reading the info on the screen
and begins slowly growing bigger and bigger...

> UNCLE ROMEO
> Because *you're* the one most likely to bring out the
> *queen* in her, whereas *he's* the one most likely to bring
> out the *fool* in her. I'm pretty sure she's the type who
> prefers to be a queen. And you may be a bit *zealously*
> dominating sometimes, Sammy, but Nick's *ridiculously*
> manipulative. I mean, you're both good guys, but your
> knee-jerk natures are *completely* opposite. *You*
> impulsively reach up and and over for the ball-- *He*
> impulsively reaches down and under for the ball. It
> works for your friendship 'n tag team battle cause you
> balance each other out like the Yin Yang Alpha and
> Omega Power Duo.

Sammy smirks angrily, cutting his eyes and looking away, shaking his head to himself,
still mad at Nick, as Uncle Romeo rattles on.

> UNCLE ROMEO (CONT'D)

You're the fun, charismatic Warrior King-- He's the cunning, self-aware Soldier Spy. You give him the will and weapons to fight offense. He gives you the shadow and shield to fight defense. And Love gives you *both* something powerfully important to fight *for*. Which is LOVE. Real, pure, true love. But the clear, stark contrast between you 2 is what's gonna make Love see who she really wants and belongs with. So let her see you both in plain day light by lifting up the cloudy veil of prohibition. Instead of making Nick The Sexy Outlaw-- or a Sympathetic Underdog, bring him back inside the house, invite him to the table. Show Love how he's your *best* brother, more *now* than *ever*. That'll not only *defuse* any sexual tension between them, and help her see you 2 more clearly, but it'll confuse the crap out of her about Nick, make her feel *VERY* uncomfortable with the idea of ping-ponging back 'n forth between you two, and show her you're the better choice for her-- cause you're the king she's been waiting for.

                SAMMY KING
          (deliberating)
I don't-- want to-- do that, Uncle Romeo.

                UNCLE ROMEO
We all have to do things we don't want to sometimes, Sammy. It's called *Working For The Greater Good.*

                SAMMY KING
Lemme rephrase that-- I don't know *how* to do that, Uncle Rome. I can't jus-- *stand back* and let her-- *fall* into his arms. I just-- *can't.*

                UNCLE ROMEO
          (leans in, intently)
Do it any way. It's called *Playing To Your Strengths*, Sammy. *Nick's* strength is sneaking in through the *back* door. Or *crying* his way in. *Your* strength is bulldozing down the *front* door. Or *charming* your way in. Either way, while he's trying to get Love at the *back* door, with Hidden Forbidden Romance and Precious Puppy Pouts, you need to be getting Love at the *front* door, with Funny Sunny *Friendship* and The Charming Happy *Warrior's Wink.*

His desk phone stops growing, then starts spinning so fast it almost looks still, until it finally stops abruptly, as if it's finished processing.

                    SAMMY KING
          And that'll work?

                    UNCLE ROMEO
               (nods)
          That'll work. Now I just gave you the best victory
          blueprint strategy and game plan to make the love of
          your life choose you over your best friend who's like a
          son to me, like you are to me. How's that for *fair?*

Deflated Sammy anxiously chuckles with hopeful uncertainty.

INT. CHURCH - YOUTH CENTER - BRIDAL ROOM - SAME

Half-naked Nick kisses Love's cheek and neck as he wraps her legs around him. Love glances up at the fluorescent ceiling lights above them, just as they stop moving like organisms and a tentacle slithers out of view. Not sure she saw anything, she pouts at herself, guilty.

                    LOVE JONES
          I should go back. This doesn't feel right.

                    NICK O' BRIEN
          Feels right to me.
               (kissing her)

                    LOVE JONES
               (lost in thought)
          When did I become a bad person?

                    NICK O' BRIEN
          You're not bad-- just confused.
               (kissing her)
          Like all the emaciated pasty Barbie doll characters in
          movies and TV shows,
               (kissing her)
          who *all* types of amazing guys fight over and call
          beautiful, while they
               (kissing her)
          do whatever ugly, frosty, selfish thing they want, all the
          time--
               (kissing her)

but everybody still calls them a beautiful, innocent,
perfect, loving, fragile, angel princess, only--
            (kissing her)
you really *are* beautiful, innocent 'n perfect, my
brilliant, loving, fragile, angel princess.
            (kissing her)
Even though you never hear it enough.
            (kissing her)
You are.
            (kissing her)
You're beautiful--
            (kissing her)
--innocent--
            (kissing her)
--and perfect.
            (kissing her)
You're jus confused.
            (kissing her)
Now I'll help you clear up that confusion.

Love abruptly pushes Nick to stop and eyes him skeptically.

                    LOVE JONES
Wait-- *Clear up my confusion?* I thought you were
suicidal.

                    NICK O' BRIEN
            (trying to look sad)
Oh, yeah... I am-- *Whatever*.

                    LOVE JONES
            (raises an eyebrow)
You don't sound suicidal, Nick.

                    NICK O' BRIEN
Oh, cause, yeah, cause-- you saved me. You-- helped
me through it. I mean-- *this* is helping me through it. I'm
sure-- I won't-- wanna kill myself-- soon as we're done
here.

                    LOVE JONES
We're done here.

She pushes him to sit up, gets up and moves toward door with folded arms, as the clock
on the wall organically mutates. He pouts at her.

                    NICK O' BRIEN

But... we only just got started...

LOVE JONES
On *what*, Nick? You *manipulating* me?

NICK O′ BRIEN
I wasn't--

LOVE JONES
Ya know, I do like you, Nick. I do love you too. And I do feel equally obligated to you because I met you as my Secret Admirer first. But I spend enough time being manipulated and lied to by everyone in my life. I don't want yet another relationship full of shady secrets 'n lies 'n passive-aggressive manipulation. If I can't trust you, I don't want you. And if you can't get me without lying or manipulating me, then maybe you don't deserve me, or we're just not meant to be together. I mean, have you ever even *had* suicidal thoughts before? Or thought bad things about yourself? Or been degraded by your step-dad like that before?

NICK O′ BRIEN
(sighs, honest)
My step-dad berates me like that almost whenever he sees me. Which is never, now, because I moved out when I was 15. Till then, I had to practically *live* here at the youth center with Sammy and Uncle Romeo, when we weren't out touring the world. Back when I lived at home, I did start to believe what my step-dad said. Especially before we got famous. Because my real dad is--
(sighs, hiding anger)
I duwanna talk about my real dad. But, jus-- all of it made me insecure and distrusting. And I may not have a long history of suicidal thoughts-- but I've very often fantasized about offing my step-dad and birth uncle.

Love stares at careful Nick in silence.

LOVE JONES
Wow. That sounds like you might actually be telling me the truth for once.

NICK O′ BRIEN
I am telling you the truth. For once.

                    LOVE JONES
                (stares at him a beat)
I'm really sorry that happened to you, Nick. You're a
great guy. But I feel like I'm gonna have to pick 1 of
you 2 pretty soon and stick with it, and I can't pick you
just because you keep making me feel bad for you.

                    NICK O′ BRIEN
I already know you're gonna pick Sammy. *The Prom
King.*

                    LOVE JONES
                (stunned)
What? Well if you're so sure of that then why are you in
here trying to get closer to me?

                    NICK O′ BRIEN
Cause I've spent almost 4 years in love with you, Love.
I'm not gonna jus *back down* from the *fight* for you.
Even if it's a losing one.

Love eyes him curiously, then goes over and sits beside him.

                    LOVE JONES
I know what it's like to feel hurt, cheated, 'n betrayed. I
don't want to make either of you feel that. I don't wanna
hurt either of you.

                    NICK O′ BRIEN
                (smiles sincerely)
Love-- me 'n Sammy've been world famous heart-
breakers for years. It's only fair that we get a broken
heart every now and then. Heartbreak is like our
Kryptonite. It keeps us in check. Reminds us that we're
human.

                    LOVE JONES
                (giggling)
K, but ya know Superman's not human, right? He's an
alien. From Planet Krypton.

                    NICK O′ BRIEN
                (feigning a Eureka)
Ah. So maybe the aliens that invaded us today-- jus
wanna stop crime, rescue kittens, and *save* us from
ourselves *too* then...

                         LOVE JONES
                          (chuckles)
              Or maybe they want to eat us for *dinner*.

                        NICK O′BRIEN
              Ah well you do look *delicious*.

He teases her. She giggles, pulling away, but he pulls her back in and kisses her softly. A
big alien tentacle peeks out from behind them and slowly rises above the couch.
Suddenly, the door opens, bringing with it loud chatter, and the tentacle abruptly shrinks
back out of view, as Love gasps and Nick looks for his shirt. Aunt Juliet enters, laughing
with another woman, who follows her in, looking anxious and hopeful.

                        AUNT JULIET
              Oh no, girl. I just have to keep my loaned-out wedding
              donations locked up in here cause I horde everything, so
              there's no room at the inn back home unfortunately, to--
                          (stops, seeing Nick)
              Nick--

                        NICK O′BRIEN
              Hi Aunt Juliet--

Nick sounds sheepish as he finds his shirt and throws it on. Love snaps her head around
at him, alarmed and embarrassed now.

                         LOVE JONES
              This is Aunt Juliet?

Nick stops to look at Love, realizing the embarrassed disenchantment in her voice, and
looks back at Aunt Juliet with an oops-like gulp for being the one to introduce Love to
one of his and Sammy's mentors in such a questionable fashion.

                        NICK O′BRIEN
              Uh, we'll jus get outta your way here.

He gets up, offers Love a hand, helping her up. She follows him toward Aunt Juliet and
the star-struck woman behind her. But Aunt Juliet stops him as Love starts to study her,
eyeing Juliet's face, hair, body, personality and mannerisms, and seeing how much Juliet
resembles her, or rather, how much Love resembles Aunt Juliet. Love's face drops in
sadly stunned realization and embarrassment.

                        AUNT JULIET
              Wait-- who's this? I didn't know you had a girlfriend.
              You didn't ask for advice on *her*.

                        NICK O′BRIEN

(sighs, knowingly)
I did, actually. Since 9th grade. Aunt Juliet, *this*-- is
Love Jones.

                    AUNT JULIET
                     (shocked)
THE-- Love Jones?

Nick nods. Juliet eyes Love in surprised awe. Love looks between them, politely, and
courteously puts her hand out for a shake.

                    LOVE JONES
Hi Miss Juliet. Nice to meet you.

                    AUNT JULIET
               (shakes hand, startled)
Hello in deed. Nice to finally meet The Legend. These
boys adore you. Does-- Sammy know you two are--
here?

                    NICK O' BRIEN
He knows *she's* here.

                    AUNT JULIET
                (nods, eyes Love)
Number two. No wonder you boys had that epic viral
video fight at school today.

                    NICK O' BRIEN
                     (confused)
What?

                    LOVE JONES
They figured out the numbers on our faces. Our *chins*
show how many people we've had *natural* consensual
sex with. Our *noses* show how many people we've had
unnatural consensual sex with. And our *foreheads* show
how many people we've ever actually *loved.*
Romantically.

                    NICK O' BRIEN
                     (stunned)
Whoa-- *Why?* Wait-- So then-- you really *do* love me
too! *Awesome...*

Love and Aunt Juliet both crack a goofy girly giggle at him the same way, and it endears
Juliet, but it only adds to the weirded out sadness starting to take over Love's demeanor.

                              NICK O′ BRIEN (CONT'D)
             Wait-- so then, what do the numbers on our cheeks
             mean?

Aunt Juliet and the wedding woman trade knowing glances.

                              AUNT JULIET
             We're not 100%, but we're pretty sure-- the left cheek
             number is how many people have violated you, and the
             right cheek number is how many people you have
             violated.

Nick and Love both look suddenly awakened, recalling people they spoke to today who
had numbers on their cheeks. Like the #3 on the Receptionist Cynthia's left cheek. Nick
gasps.

                              NICK O′ BRIEN
             Oh my God-- Deville had like 666 on his right cheek.
             That's like one victim every week for 14 years straight.

                              LOVE JONES
                         (calculates in her head)
             Or two a month for 28 years.

                              NICK O′ BRIEN
                         (stricken by it)
             Dude... We been hangin' out with *monsters*. --Does
             Sammy know?

                              SAMMY KING
             Does Sammy know what?

Sammy saunters into the room, eyes the 2 of them sternly... then tries to lighten up. Uncle
Romeo follows him in, smiles at his wife and kisses her sweetly on the cheek.

                              UNCLE ROMEO
             Hey sweety.

                              AUNT JULIET
             Hey sweety.

Love admires the stable and loving nature of their relationship. She looks down, starting
to realize.

                              NICK O′ BRIEN
             Our manager's a serial rapist.

SAMMY KING
(alarmed)
What??

NICK O' BRIEN
(points to his own face)
Our left cheek is who raped us, our right cheek is who
we raped, and Deville's got like almost 700 victims on
his right cheek.

SAMMY KING
(shaking his head)
Nah, that's not right. I mean... he's a ridiculous person 'n
all, but... that's just straight-up *hyper-psychotic.*

LOVE JONES
Sammy-- we need to talk.

NICK O' BRIEN
(grins triumphantly)
Uh oh. That's never a good starting line!

SAMMY KING
Love-- before you say it-- I already know whassup, so I
want you to know-- I approve of you having your way
with Nick, and then coming back to settle down with
me.

LOVE JONES
(lost offended shock)
What??

SAMMY KING
(to Uncle Romeo)
Did that come out wrong?

UNCLE ROMEO
(briskly nods in awe)
VERY wrong.

SAMMY KING
(back to Love)
OK-- I meant-- You have my full authorization to do
whatever you want with Nick-- so you-- can figure out
which one of us you like more.

LOVE JONES

(weirded out)
Huh?

                    SAMMY KING
          (sighs, frustrated)
Nick's taking you home tonight. I guess.

                    NICK O′ BRIEN
          (excited)
I am?

                    LOVE JONES
No one's taking me. I'm going home alone. I'll call for a
ride home. Nice to meet you all.

Love whisks out of room, confusing everyone. Sammy glares at Nick.

                    SAMMY KING
What did you do-- AGAIN?

                    NICK O′ BRIEN
          (shrugs)
Nothin'. I was a perfect gentleman.

                    SAMMY KING
You mean a *crying* gentleman.

                    NICK O′ BRIEN
Perfect, crying, whatever. Either way I was good at it,
and she was happy, until you came in the room.

                    AUNT JULIET
Actually, until *I* came in the room. Sammy-- did you
ever show Love a picture of me?

                    SAMMY KING
Yeah. Same one we show everyone.

                    AUNT JULIET
That's not very clear. I mean, you ever show her a close-
up?

                    SAMMY KING
No, why?

                    AUNT JULIET
I think ya better hear it from her.

Sammy looks confused, glances at Nick, then back at his Aunt and Uncle with a solemn nod, turns, and goes after Love. Nick follows. Everyone stares after them.

                    AUNT JULIET (CONT'D)
          Well this turned into some crazy drama.

                    UNCLE ROMEO
          Yeah and that's *before* we get to the *aliens*.

Aunt Juliet and the woman chuckle.

INT. CHURCH - YOUTH CENTER - OFFICE HALLWAY - SAME

Sammy sees Love sitting on stoop outside, through glass door. He heads toward her, but stops when he notices Nick trailing him. Sammy turns and pushes Nick back with one hand.

                    SAMMY KING
          I got this.

                    NICK O' BRIEN
          Yeah well maybe I got this too.

                    SAMMY KING (V.O.)
          Like hell you do.

                    SAMMY KING
          Nick-- every time you get involved, things get worse. So
          I'll handle her this time. You can handle her *next* time--
          How 'bout that?

Sammy shakes his head in annoyance at Nick and whips on down the hall, bopping out of the door, as Nick pouts humorously.

                    NICK O' BRIEN
          But *I* wanna handle her *now*.

EXT. CHURCH - YOUTH CENTER - BACK STOOP - SAME

Sammy sits by Love and nudges her playfully with his shoulder, as she buries her face in her knees, with her arms around her legs.

                    SAMMY KING
          How's my favorite cupcake doing?
                    (hears sniffles)
          Heyyy, what's wrong? Why ya cryin'?

He drapes an arm around her back and cups the palm of his hand over hers, rubbing her fingers with urgent concern in his voice and face, despite his relaxed body language.

                    LOVE JONES
          This is all too much for me, Sammy. I can't deal with it.
          I jus can't.

                    SAMMY KING
     Aw, sweety--

He wraps her in a giant bear hug as she cries on his shoulder, trying not to chuckle boyishly at her overwhelmed meltdown.

                    SAMMY KING (CONT'D)
          It's OK. It'll be OK. You're OK.

                    LOVE JONES
          It's not OK.
                    (pulls away from him)
          I can't be with you.

                    SAMMY KING
                    (shocked)
          You're choosing *Nick?*

                    LOVE JONES
                    (shaking head)
          I can't be with him either.

                    SAMMY KING
                    (confused)
          There's a *3rd* guy?

                    SAMMY KING (V.O.)
          I thought the only guy in her life was *Kyle...*

                    LOVE JONES
          There's nobody. Just you two. And I can't do this. Even
          if I'm wrong and I'm safe in your world-- It doesn't
          matter, cause you guys don't really love *me.* You love
          some weird whimsical shared *fantasy* idea of your Aunt
          Juliet that you're just projecting onto me.

                    SAMMY KING
                    (stunned)
          What? What are you talkin' about?

LOVE JONES

You really don't see it? We look like long-lost relatives, Sammy. We're definitely from the same tribe. My "tall, thick, voluptuous body"? Check. My "sweet, innocent angel face"? Check. My big, fluffy, curly, Scary Spice Girl hair? Check. Even my cheerful, perky personality, goofy girly mannerisms and signature endangered species values-- Check check and check. I'm the teen version of *her*. Dude-- I'm her friggin' *Mini Me!*

SAMMY KING
(realizes, laughs)
Huh. Yeah I guess you two do have a lot in common, come to think of it.

LOVE JONES

Which is the *real* reason why you guys even *noticed* me back in 9th grade. It wasn't just my fliers. It was my doppelganger value. You saw your Aunt Juliet in me. And I get it. You admire your Uncle Romeo. He's the man who showed you both how to be men. So you wanna be like him. He has a beautiful wife. Happy, loving relationship. The perfect family. And you wanna be like that. So you admire *Aunt Juliet*, as like, the ideal woman, who-- I guess, encompasses everything you want in a girl. So you wanna find someone just like her. That's-- understandable, Sammy. But-- I'm not her. I can't live up to your idea of her. I'm not even sure *she* can, so I *know I can't.* I mean she's a good person to set the bar, I see why she's your fantasy. And I know *most* girls have to fight against being expected to live up to perverted, *disgusting* male fantasies that shouldn't even *exist*, wheres at least this one's a wholesome and *admirable* one. But *any* fantasy is impossible to live up to. You guys are both gonna fall out of love with me as soon as it finally hits you that I'm not her.

SAMMY KING
(laughs to himself)
Love-- if I were you, I would look at the glass half full. Even if it was true, which it's not, it should only give you more confidence, not less. You should be like--
(mocks diva queen)
Yeah that's right. I'm The Perky Princess and I got 2 hot rock 'n jock celebrity heartthrobs in love and obsessed with me cause I look 'n act like their ideal woman. Yeah

*I got em sprung like chung 'n can't no other girl in the
world top this rung!*

She laughs at his funny interpretation of a bad-ass Queen B, as he laughingly snaps his
fingers and rolls his neck. He smiles warmly at her as she hugs his arm, still giggling.

                SAMMY KING (CONT'D)
See? Glass half-full, Love. Always. Now-- I'm sorry
your 1 amazing Secret Admirer turned out to be *both* of
us. But my life was jus way too hectic to introduce you
to it back then. Even I was still adjusting to it. And then
my fans kept mauling each other like sex-crazed
animals, attacking any girl they thought I was with.
Except for Holly-- who they were afraid of. So I had to
protect you from them.

                LOVE JONES
Is that only who you were protecting me from? Your
fans?

                SAMMY KING
            (confused by her)
Well, yeah. Who else?

                LOVE JONES
            (eyes him seriously)
Sammy, are ya sure, deep down, what you were really
afraid of happening to me wasn't just WHAT happened
to Cynthia-- but WHO? I mean like, are you sure you
weren't afraid of *other* people in your show biz world
preying on me, like they may have preyed on every
other show biz kid or friends you knew?

                SAMMY KING
            (shrugs)
Yeah there's a lotta creeps 'n psychos in Hollywood and
the music industry, Love, but I can protect you from all
that.

                LOVE JONES
Yeah *now*, maybe. *MAYBE.* But, you're still closely
managed by 1 of the biggest predators of them all.

                SAMMY KING
Whaya talkin' about? Deville? Nah. He's a greedy
weasel who'll do anything for a buck, but I never seen
him physically hurt anyone.

SAMMY KING (V.O.)
Whoa-- wait-- *what?*

Sammy's eyes flit wide with a slack jaw, stunned by the horrific thought. He shakes his head to himself.

LOVE JONES
Well I never really met him. Just seen him runnin' around school, trackin' you down or talkin' on his phone. But in less than an hour I heard his name twice around the same shady biz. *Nick* says he has Rape-Face. *You* say he's one of your show biz peeps Cynthia met, before she went spiraling out of control. Then I recall seeing a number 3 on her left cheek. Three guesses as to which one of her violators was your career manager, Deville?

SAMMY KING (V.O.)
Whoa-- wait-- *what?*

Sammy's eyes flit wide with a slack jaw, stunned by the horrific thought. He shakes his head to himself.

SAMMY KING
No... can't be. He's not that bad. She-- She-- She woulda told me-- that.

LOVE JONES
Would she? If he threatened her life, or her relationship with you, or your life and career, saying he would make her the most hated girl in the world for making you lose all your fame, fortune and fans, the way she accused me of doing? I can see all that being a very convincing threat to keep a 13 or 14 year old's mouth shut. And then if he paid her off too... Did she mysteriously trip into a windfall of money after you two broke up?

SAMMY KING
(thinks, realizing)
No, I-- Wait... Well she was working class when we met. Then she kept showing off pics of her new cars 'n jewelry on Facebook, after she got out of rehab. I just thought she got an endorsement deal for tellin' the world what it was like to date me. Then it all died down 'n she went back to normal life.

LOVE JONES
You mean the hush money ran out.

SAMMY KING
(holds head in shock)
A lot of people I know suddenly come into money after being in my life. I just thought it was cause I took pics wit them or whatever and it made them a paid influencer

on YouTube or something. Or a paid source for tabloids.
Cause that happens a lot.

LOVE JONES

If Nick's idea of Deville's face is true-- your manager
has probably raped at least 1 out of every 5 girls who
got close to you. Probably more. Targeting poor girls,
fast girls, and desperate girls who adore you and don't
wanna rock the boat or get "handled". In other words--
Easy Targets.

SAMMY KING (V.O.)

Jesus save our souls-- *Is she right?*

SAMMY KING
(speechlessly rattled)
That scumbag-demon-spawn-cockroach motha-- I'll kill
him. Then break his legs.
(thinks, realizes)
Err, no, wait-- I'll break his legs first-- and *then* I'll kill
him.

LOVE JONES

Right. And all during a weird, creepy alien invasion.
Good luck wit that. I'm going home.

She gets up and walks past him. He gets up and stops her.

SAMMY KING

Wait-- Love-- We can work this out.

LOVE JONES
(shakes head, tearful)
Sammy-- I can't.

SAMMY KING
(at a loss)
But-- Don't you *want* me?

LOVE JONES

Of course I *want* you, Sammy. But you know what I
don't want? I don't wanna be like your ex-girlfriend
Cynthia-- who, by the way, judging by the #1 on her
forehead, is probably still in love with you, Sammy.
Maybe cause you showed her wholesome kindness
when no one else would. I dunno. But I just-- I just-- I
just don't--

(huff-sighs)
I *don't* want to *compete* with your *aunt*. I *don't* want to
get *stabbed* by your *fans*. I *don't* want to get *raped* by
your *manager*. I *don't* want to become the *Yoko Ono
breaker upper* of your *band*. And I *don't* want to *be* the
wrecking ball that ruins the best, most *famous* friendship
of all time, the *legendary* duo of Nick O'Brien and
Sammy King. And how much I *do* want you, or Nick, or
my own fun, freedom and filthy rich fantasies-- can't
cancel out how much I *don't* want the hellish *nightmare*
and endless *guilt* that follows it.

                  SAMMY KING
(holds her hand)
Love, I'll get rid of Deville. I'll keep you safe, stay
friends with Nick and our band, and-- I never wanted
you to compete with my aunt. So why start now? I love
you, you love me, we're good for each other. No reason
we can't make it work. So what's on your mind? Tell me
what else is really bothering you.

Love sighs, looks down, then back at him, eyes glistening.

                  LOVE JONES
Sammy, we are the youth of the nation and we live in a
society that doesn't love us, doesn't care about us, and
doesn't even *think* about us unless it relates to *using* us
for *money* and *political* power, or *exploiting* us for *sex*.
The rich, powerful elites who run our society don't care
about us *spiritually,* when it comes to finding God and
valuing our purity-- *mentally,* when it comes to
developing our critical thinking 'n original thought--
emotionally, when it comes to protecting our
psychological health and us learning how to build better,
realer, more *lasting* relationships-- *morally*, when it
comes to teaching us right from wrong and then doing
right by us. And even *physically*-- when it comes to
guarding our bodies and safety. They pump us full of
messed up, hormone-injected food *product* that gives
men *tits* and makes *boys* want to be *girls* and *vice versa*.
Then they shove a bunch of suicidal side-effected,
pharmaceutical-grade prescription drugs down our
throats to pretend to fix what they *knowingly* broke.
Then they imprison us together in either *actual* prisons,
if you're an economically challenged boy of visible
ethnicity, *or* they imprison us together in the *poorly*

funded STD-factory zoos they call *schools,* where all
they do is tell us what we *"can't wear"* and throw
condoms in our faces, before we get *bullied* to death out
in the school halls.

Sammy chuckles with a knowing nod of agreeing solidarity.

                    LOVE JONES (CONT'D)
Meanwhile, they push nonstop constant 24/7 promotion
of sleazy, filthy, trashy, twisted, sick, disturbing,
perverted mass media pop culture. From stripper music
to porno movies and perv TV. Which inspires
*EVERYONE to prey on us like LAMBS groomed for
SLAUGHTER.* The greedy, sleepy adults running our
society not only don't care about finding and stopping
the predators who were "born that way", but they get
paid to mold minds to morph into monsters that
wouldn't have even otherwise existed if it wasn't for our
sick, psychotically sex-crazed, morally bankrupt society.
All the pedophiles, child molesters, rapists and show biz
execs or writers out there over-sexualizing us as soon as
we pop out of the womb-- devouring our spirits and
defiling our souls before we're even aware they're there-
- and nobody does anything about it, because nobody
who ever notices or cares has the money and power to
fix it, and nobody who has the money and power to fix
it ever notices or cares.

Sammy looks down and gulps slightly, clearly feeling guilty.

                    SAMMY KING (V.O.)
Couldn't agree more. But wow. I got the money and
power to help fix it. And I didn't. Now-- here, the love
of my life, is ranting on about her moral-cultural lament-
- a lament my career choices have helped to deepen.

                    LOVE JONES
So the rich and powerful elites jus keep feeding the
monster, green-lighting predators, by monotonously
manufacturing a godless, soulless, psychotic pop
culture, that psychologically trains adults to prey on us,
like Anna's statutory rapist, Paula's dad, and Cynthia's
attacker-- your *show biz* manager-- and psychologically
trains *us* to prey on *each other*, like Spykult and Holly.
They *create* the predators. They put us in the *path* of the
predators. Then they don't even bother to *warn* us and
say to us, "Oh hey! That guy or girl is probably a

predator-- or *might* be-- so you should probably *stay the hell away from them*".

She huffs, frustrated and sad. Sammy gazes at her in her deep-rooted upset with new understanding and sincere sympathy.

> LOVE JONES (CONT'D)
> Sammy-- I live in a culture so the *opposite* of me and everything I stand for-- I can't even stomach it any more. And now I realize it's the same world that you-- *my 4 year Secret Admirer*-- live and work in. A world that *you* learned to navigate so ingeniously in, for yourself. But-- *I'm not you,* Sammy. Or Nick. Your world wants to destroy anyone like me. Proudly. Swiftly. Totally. I dunno how to survive it. And you can't protect me from all the 50 million demons circling you and Nick, demons both you guys *somehow* managed to elude for so long. It's jus not possible.

She sighs, accepting defeat. Sammy studies her carefully.

> SAMMY KING (V.O.)
> OK, but what does she need from me that I can give her *right now*-- to get rid of her fear and torment?

> LOVE JONES
> Like I said-- I really do want you-- *so* bad, Sammy. But I don't wanna be compared to an unrequited fantasy. I don't wanna get shanked by your groupies. I don't wanna be violated by your colleagues. I don't wanna get internationally known on the microphone for forcing your famously fun band into early retirement. And I don't wanna be the crack that breaks the glass crystal kingdom known as the legendary friendship of Nick O'Brien and Sammy King. And to top it all off, we're being invaded by-- *Valentine Aliens*-- who are *bizarrely* obsessed with our sex and love lives?! Yeah-- No-- I can't do this, Sammy. It's just-- WAY too much. Too scary and too overwhelming. I just-- *can't.*

She quickly turns and rushes off. He chases after her, both of them turning a corner. He grabs her hand, stops her, backs her up against a building wall and kisses her. At 1st she tries to push him away, shaking her head at him, but he holds her in place, and the longer he kisses her, the more she softens and kisses him back, enraptured, weak in the knees, and wanting more. Then he looks into her intoxicated eyes.

SAMMY KING

You feel alone. You've felt morally and culturally alone your whole life, like a generational misfit, whose mere existence goes against the grain-- I get it. I feel you. I'm with you. I felt the same way as you. Nick felt the same way as you. Only we had each other, and a shared game-plan to hoodwink the world into bowing at our feet, in exchange for keeping the true light inside of us a secret. And sin aside, we jus shouldn't have kept you in the dark all that time. We should've at least brought you into the loop, even though you woulda never agreed with it. But we didn't. So now, on top of facing years of feeling like an alien-- you're scared and overwhelmed by all this. OK, Love. I get it. I feel you. I'm with you. Me too. I'm scared n overwhelmed too. Like you.

LOVE JONES
(sucks teeth, looking away,
shaking head)
No you're not. You're just mirroring me to get me to agree with you. Like they taught us in Sales & Commerce Class 101. You're not a mess like I am, Sammy. You never are.

SAMMY KING

Of course I am, Love. I see the madness all around us. Most of it I have no control over. Every day, I face the fact I feel alone in my family, alone in my fame. Then I find out my best friend-- my brother-- the bro-lifeline to my inner solidarity-- has been secretly loving the love of my life behind my back for 4 years? I am *very* freaked and stressed out about it all right now, Love. But in addition to my faith and fortitude, you know what keeps me centered and sane through it all?

LOVE JONES

What?

SAMMY KING

Knowing I have you. Knowing that as a team, we can face the odds together and conquer any monsters that come our way-- *together.* Because *that's* how you survive, rise up, and change the world. By joining hands *together,* with the people who'll stand by your side in war, and go to battle for you. And Love, I'm telling you. I will fight for you. I will live for you, I will die for you,

I will fight for you-- now and always. You are not alone.
Ya were never alone. I got ya back, baby. I got you.

Love turns away to hide her tears, but Sammy holds her face gently, in the palms of his
hands, rubbing her cheeks softly with his thumbs, as she silently breaks down before him.

                    SAMMY KING (CONT'D)
And I'm sorry-- I am *so* sorry for lying about my values
to get rich and famous. Putting on a mask that wasn't
who I am or want to be. Selfishly feeding the monster
that deepens your moral lament. I stopped adding to the
solution and started adding to the problems plaguing our
generation, our goodness, and our truth. And I'm sorry I
didn't have the courage to be brave like you. But now
that we're together I *will* work on it. Cause you're right.
The world is crumbling right in front of us. But I'm not
asking you to have faith in the world. I'm askin' you to
have faith in *me.*
          (nods at her)
Can you do that for me, baby? Can ya jus-- have a little
faith in me?

Love gazes back at him carefully as another tear cascades down her cheek. She nods at
him, as if not wanting to want to, but unable to stop herself. He smiles warmly at her.

                    SAMMY KING (CONT'D)
That's my girl. My Love.

He pulls her in for a warm embrace and Love sinks into his arms, breathing relief into his
chest, as she closes her eyes in emotional exhaustion. Sammy looks off into the distance,
as he hugs Love-- and he sees the giant golden alien monster that they saw back in the
school locker room, just standing there, staring at them from the big, wide, grassy church
yard. It gradually becomes invisible, slowly disappearing from sight. Sammy urgently
furrows his brow at this and hugs Love even tighter, in new thoughtfully concerned
silence.

                    SAMMY KING (V.O.)
What do they want from us?

INT. CEKKSEATENE HIGH SCHOOL - HALLS - NEXT DAY

Various teens chat loudly, up and down the halls, in animated frenzy. Holly glares
maniacally at Love, who giggles excitedly with her friends, in between texting on her
phone. Molly curls her tongue around the top of her top lip as she takes a sexy selfie of
herself on her phone and Dolly reads the school news on her phone with a gasp. None of
them notice that their devices are living organisms with hidden eyes now.

                    DOLLY MANDY JESSICA SWIFT
Oh my GOD-- Did you guys hear about The
Overachievers Club? Ms. Reddit, The Librarian, said
she saw them having a meeting upstairs in the library
over by the elevator and bathrooms, then suddenly she
heard screaming, and when she went to see what
happened, they were gone. As in, like, *disappeared.*
And *no one's seen them since.*

                    HOLLY WOOD
Only *you* would care about what happens to some
library nerds, Dolly.

                    MOLLY PARIS PAMELA KARDASHIAN
                    (snapping selfie pix)
Yeah, why should *we* care?

                    DOLLY MANDY JESSICA SWIFT
                    (shocked)
Because it might have something to do with the *aliens*--
DUH.

                    MOLLY PARIS PAMELA KARDASHIAN

What aliens?

                    DOLLY MANDY JESSICA SWIFT
The *Valentine* Aliens-- That's what Sammy called them
in his viral video news clip...

                    MOLLY PARIS PAMELA KARDASHIAN
Who are *The Valentine Aliens?* Have I heard any of
their songs?

                    DOLLY MANDY JESSICA SWIFT
                    (stares at her)
Molly Paris Pamela Kardashian-- you can *NOT* be
serious.

                    MOLLY PARIS PAMELA KARDASHIAN
                    (gawks briefly at her)
Dolly Mandy Jessica Swift-- *WHAT* are you talking
about?

                    DOLLY MANDY JESSICA SWIFT
                    (disbelief)
Molly! You *do* know there are *aliens* hovering over
school right now right? They've been occupying our

entire planet since yesterday afternoon. Hello--
NUMBERS ON OUR FACES?

She points bluntly to the numbers on her face. Molly smirks.

> MOLLY PARIS PAMELA KARDASHIAN
> Oh yeah. Wonder if Valentine Aliens rate selfies. Like if
> they like all my porno Twit-pix better than anyone
> else's. I think they're hot.

> DOLLY MANDY JESSICA SWIFT
> (disbelief)
> Why am I friends with you?

> HOLLY WOOD
> (snaps neck at her)
> Because deep down Dolly, you're a shy, insecure,
> mousy little *science geek,* who's *lucky* to have *boss
> bitches* like us in her life to give you a *makeover,* make
> you look like 1 of the *glamorous popular* kids and save
> you from the boring *weakness* of sad nerdy *obscurity.*
> And you know if it wasn't for your name rhyming with
> ours, we ***prolly*** wouldn't be so kind. So *I* made you--
> and *I* can *break* you. That's why we're your best friends.
> Now shut up about The Stupid Overachievers Club, take
> your flamin' red ginger ass to the teacher's lounge, and
> get me another latte.

Holly shoves her tumbler into Dolly's stomach. Dolly grabs it to get it off of her and
scoffs at Holly, folding her arms.

> DOLLY MANDY JESSICA SWIFT
> I'm not your *bitch,* Holly Wood.

> HOLLY WOOD
> (smirks wickedly)
> Molly-- gimme the keys.

> MOLLY PARIS PAMELA KARDASHIAN
> (still taking selfies)
> What keys?

> HOLLY WOOD
> The *janitor's* keys. Duh.

> MOLLY PARIS PAMELA KARDASHIAN

Oh yeah. They're in my locker. I'll get 'em after I'm
done.

                    DOLLY MANDY JESSICA SWIFT
Why'd you take the janitor's keys?

                    HOLLY WOOD
That would be *none* of your business.

                    DOLLY MANDY JESSICA SWIFT
It's *my* business if it's *Molly's* business.

                    HOLLY WOOD
I'm not telling her either, until it's time to bring you both
in. But I need the keys 1st and she's sleeping with the
janitor, so--

                    DOLLY MANDY JESSICA SWIFT
          (stunned, disgusted)
Wait-- You slept with the *janitor?*

                    MOLLY PARIS PAMELA KARDASHIAN
Yeah? So?

                    DOLLY MANDY JESSICA SWIFT
Oh my God-- *Why?*

                    MOLLY PARIS PAMELA KARDASHIAN
He retweeted 1 of my sexy naked pix.

                    DOLLY MANDY JESSICA SWIFT
You slept with him-- cause he retweeted you.

                    MOLLY PARIS PAMELA KARDASHIAN
          (still selfie-posing)
Uh huh.

                    DOLLY MANDY JESSICA SWIFT
Wow, Molly. Just-- *Wow.*

                    MOLLY PARIS PAMELA KARDASHIAN
I know, *right?* I didn't know the janitor was *following*
me!

Dolly just stares at her in grossed out awe. Holly sees this and smacks her shoulder,
incensed by her sexual standards.

HOLLY WOOD

Oh don't act like you're new. You knew she was a whore last year when she slept with the whole frigging football team and then posted it on Instagram. She hasn't changed, so what has? You been actin' different ever since you saw Sammy King and Nick O'Brien ferociously fist fight for the love of their *precious* lil *virgin*. Got somethin' to confess?

DOLLY MANDY JESSICA SWIFT
(blushes, alarmed)

What? No, no. I-- I just thought Molly could do a lil better than a creepy old guy. Like-- maybe a hot teacher or something, heheh.

MOLLY PARIS PAMELA KARDASHIAN

We don't have any hot teachers.

HOLLY WOOD
(smells Dolly's fear)

Oh is that all? When *was* the last time you got laid, Dolly? Last time you wowed us with all the stories of all your wild sexcapades with that hot college guy who you showed us pictures of was like-- last *year*.

DOLLY MANDY JESSICA SWIFT

That was last *month*.

HOLLY WOOD

Oh. Feels like an eternity. By the way-- when do we finally get to meet this hot sexy stud-muffin, Dolly? Kinda weird for you to be *goin' steady, all hot 'n heavy* wit this great cute amazing guy, yet-- you've never once introduced him to any of your 2 best friends.

DOLLY MANDY JESSICA SWIFT
(gulps, then shrugs)

I-- jus don't want you 2 heifers stealin' him away from me. Is all.

HOLLY WOOD
(staring knowingly)

Humph... Well you have a point there. We *would* steal him away from you.

She smacks Molly's arm with a mean giggle. Molly smirks.

                    MOLLY PARIS PAMELA KARDASHIAN
          Got *that* right.

Dolly laughs anxiously with them, holding Holly's tumbler. Then she looks over at PJ as
he jokes with his boys, Jimmy and Alex. She realizes he has the same numbers on his
face that she has on hers-- zeros everywhere, including their foreheads. She furrows her
brow in curiosity at this. PJ glances her way, notices and nods up at her. She gasps
slightly, blushing with butterflies, and waves discretely back at him with a shy smile.
Neither of them see alien tentacles slithering through the school vents above them. PJ
notices Nick bopping down the hall, scrolling through his phone, with his backpack
coolly slung over his shoulder, before he stops at the water fountain. PJ looks down in
serious thought. Jimmy and Alex loudly gawk at their phones, laughing as they watch
Sammy's video with reporter Kathy.

                         JIMMY SCREECH
          Oho! Sammy called them VALENTINE ALIENS and
          said NUKE. THEM. OUT! NUKE. THEM. OUT!
          NUKE. THEM. OUT!

                          ALEX MORRIS
          NUKE. THEM. OUT! NUKE. THEM. OUT! NUKE.
          THEM. OUT!

The boys chant excitedly together, throwing up rock fists with each emphasis. PJ SLAMS
his locker door shut and snaps at them.

                           PJ SLATER
          Yo why do you care what Sammy thinks?? --He's a *tool!*

Jimmy deflates to avoid any friction. But Alex ventures in.

                          ALEX MORRIS
          Hey, why do you hate Sammy so much, PJ? I mean-- I
          get he's got privileged Celebrity Status over us in class,
          but-- he's a pretty nice guy. Whad he ever do to you?

                           PJ SLATER
                            (grumpy)
          It's a long story.

                         JIMMY SCREECH
                            (shrugs)
          We got time.

                           PJ SLATER
          Not in the mood.

PJ goes back to opening his locker, fiddling with stuff inside it. Jimmy and Alex throw each other whateverish looks, shrug, shut their lockers and bounce away, into math class. PJ looks back at them. Then at Nick, who's still too busy texting on his phone to take his swig of water from the fountain. An alien tentacle tries to slither out of PJ's locker and lunge at him, right as PJ shuts his locker. He bops over to Nick who doesn't take his eyes away from his screen as he types a message and steps aside, sensing someone standing there.

                         NICK O' BRIEN
              Oh-- you can use it.

                         PJ SLATER
              Yeah, no, I-- jus-- wanted to let you know something.

                         NICK O' BRIEN
                    (looks up, sees him)
              PJ-- Heyyy...

Nick looks obviously puzzled at PJ's presence. PJ shifts awkwardly, a bit unsure of himself as well.

                         PJ SLATER
              I jus-- I jus wanted to say-- I'm-- sorry you lost ya girl--
              to Sammy. I know what it's like to want something more
              than anything in the world, and then lose it to him, and
              he doesn't even feel bad about it. He just keeps winning
              and achieving and then just-- leaves you in the dust--
              like you're nothing but his beaten competition. So--
              sorry you lost your best friend, Nick. It was inevitable.

PJ starts to walk away. Nick furrows his brow and stops him.

                         NICK O' BRIEN
              Hey-- PJ-- Wait-- Whadaya talkin' about? Whad Sammy
              take from you? I mean, I know you guys use to hang
              out, back in, like, grade school days, but-- what
              happened?

                         PJ SLATER
                    (sighs)
              It's a long story.

                         NICK O' BRIEN
              I got time.

Nick shrugs. PJ eyes him and nods with another sigh.

PJ SLATER

When I was 7, my mom took me to a musical play at a church-- Sammy's church. She liked what she saw so she took me backstage with her to give Sammy's mom her Talent Scout business card. She wanted to take Sammy with me on auditions for commercials and TV shows 'n represent him if he got somethin'. His mom didn't take my mom seriously, but she liked the idea of him having more friends besides just you, I guess. So she let my mom take Sammy to auditions with me. For a few years we would do little plays here and there together. Even do a few auditions together, going in to see the casting agents at the same time. We were like show biz brothers. Audition buddies. While you were off being his best friend in church and school, I was off being his best friend in arts and entertainment work. And we had a lotta fun. Once in a while I got something, even though it was rare. But Sammy kept knocking it outta the park every time, getting parts and winning roles... but--
              (sighs)
But my mom started discounting me from stuff, like she thought I was weaker than Sammy or something. So, I complained to my mom, who-- obviously-- liked Sammy so much better than her own son-- that I wanted her to take me on just ONE audition that she didn't tell Sammy about, so I could prove to her I was just as likable 'n bankable 'n winning as he was. I jus wanted my mom to be proud of me. Probably annoyed her to do it, but finally, she took me to an audition without telling Sammy. And I got the part.

              NICK O' BRIEN
          (nods, inspired)
That's great, PJ. What was it?

              PJ SLATER
The Grassi Mouse Camp Musical.

Suddenly Nick's countenance falls, in slow realization now.

              PJ SLATER (CONT'D)
First day of shooting, I ask my mom not to bring Sammy. But she's like, "Oh, it'll be fine. You already got the part." *Right.*
          (rolls irritated eyes)

We get there and everybody's nice. I say all my lines, hit
all my marks. But there's this 1 line of dialogue-- this
one line-- I'm having trouble remembering and saying
right. *Just one line.* I can tell the director, cast and crew
are all getting tired of having to re-shoot the same scene
over and over jus cause of this one line, and apparently
so could Sammy. So he grabs a copy of the script, runs
over to me, on set, and tells me to switch places with
him. Says something about how he remembers his lines
better when he hears them said back to him.

NICK O' BRIEN
(nods, familiar with this)
That's true.

PJ SLATER
(shrugs, rolling eyes)
Right, well, I don't know any better, so I go along with
it. He does my part and I do the other character's part.
We finish the scene, but we're still in the middle of
rehearsal, about to switch places back, when all the
sudden, I hear this loud round of applause. I look over
and see the cast and crew off to the side of the set--
giving us a standing ovation. They watched the whole
thing. I'm a kid, so I'm thinkin' they're clapping for both
of us, but next thing I know, I'm off the show and
Sammy's the new star-- all because they liked his 10
Year Old Black Swag better than my 9 Year Old one.
Then mom stops takin' me on auditions altogether, so
she can be a full-time manager for Sammy, til your guy
Deville sees Sammy's affect on people and convinces
Sammy's mom to replace my mom with himself. So I
got undermined by Sammy and what my mom still calls
to this day *"his irresistible it-factor"* and my family's
bank account still didn't even reap all the rewards of it--
cause then Deville took over.

NICK O' BRIEN
(floored)
Wow-- That really *was* a long story.

PJ SLATER
I told you.

NICK O' BRIEN

But I don't get it, PJ. After Sammy got that gig, he asked
the show-runners to bring *me 'n Mo* on, instead of
strangers, to play 2 of his fake band members, cause we
played music together in real life at church. If you 2

were friends and he knew you got the part 1st, why
wouldn't he do the same for you?

              PJ SLATER
That's the million dollar question, isn't it?

              NICK O' BRIEN
        (shakes his head)
That doesn't sound like Sammy.

              PJ SLATER
Course not. Cause Sammy's a *saint* who'd *never* do
something like-- throw you under the bus in an *epic*
viral video that *"broke the internet"* last night, just to
keep you away from what he *wanted* or anything--
right?

              NICK O' BRIEN
That's-- *way* more complicated...

              PJ SLATER
Is it?

Nick gulps to himself slightly and looks off in newly rattled thought. PJ smirks, patting
his shoulder.

              PJ SLATER (CONT'D)
Sorry for your loss, Nick. You 2 were famously great
friends. Now you just like me. Nothing but The Great
Sammy King's defeated competition, stranded in
darkness, at the deserted island of misfit ex-best-friends.
Well... Was fun while it lasted. Right?

PJ shrugs half-sincerely, half-sarcastically, then nods.

              PJ SLATER (CONT'D)
Welcome to the club, Nick.

PJ turns and bops away, into class. Nick looks down in thunder-struck new thought. Then
he sees Love chatting with her friends and texts her: *"Sorry-- got stopped by somebody.
Don't let Sammy tell you what to do. If you wanna hang with me or don't wanna hang
with either of us-- it's *your* choice. You need to let him know he has to respect that. I
wanna introduce you to my mom after school. U free?"*

Slightly further down the hall, Love's phone beeps as her friends laugh. She checks it, reading Nick's message as her friends gawk at each other over her new love life drama.

PAULA HONEY
(proudly)
I knew all along it was them.

KYLE GREEN
(deflated by loss)
You did not.

PAULA HONEY
Sure did.

ANNA KAY
When did you figure it out?

PAULA HONEY
Last year, when I caught them both staring at her at the talent show.

KYLE GREEN
Well of course they were staring. She sang beautifully and said 1 of her amazing poems.

PAULA HONEY
I mean when she was sitting and Holly was on stage, gyrating like a drunk chimpanzee. They were both still staring at Love. So I started watching them more after that and I started noticin' their body language whenever either of them were near her. It changed. I realized they were both paying her special attention without realizing it themselves. It was subtle. Not easy to notice unless you were lookin' for it. But I saw it.

ANNA KAY
Wow. Why didn't you tell us?

LOVE JONES
More like *why didn't you tell ME?*

Love chuckles with her friends as she texts Nick, *"I'm sorry but I can't. And he knows all that. I'm jus more comfortable being with 1 of you at a time, for a while, even if it changes later on down the road, like in a few months or something. Right now, I choose Sammy."* Paula shrugs.

PAULA HONEY

I dunno. Sammy's fans can get kinda stabby. I figured
they both had good reason not to tell you they were the
ones in love with you.

Nick reads text back from Love and abruptly looks up at her in upset concern. She looks
at him discretely, mouthing, *"I'm sorry"*. He huffs, not entirely accepting defeat, but still
wounded by her favor for Sam. Suddenly, Sam's pretty half-sister, Sophia, 15, pops up in
Nick's face.

                    SOPHIA KING
          Hiya Nick!

                    NICK O′ BRIEN
                         (startled)
          Oh-- Hi Sophia.

                    SOPHIA KING
          So whadayou think about these Valentine Aliens?
          Crazy, right?

                    NICK O′ BRIEN
                         (glancing at Love)
          Whah? Yeah, it's messed up.

                    SOPHIA KING
                         (eyes Love, realizes, nods to
                         herself)
          Tough break, what happened between you and my
          brother. Hope you guys can work it out and stay friends.

                    NICK O′ BRIEN
                         (distracted by Love)
          Yeah... hope so.

                    SOPHIA KING
          Yeah, so... Why don't we hang out after school? I'm free
          if you are.

                    NICK O′ BRIEN
          Huh?

Nick suddenly looks at her like he's just now fully noticing her, then he looks back at
Love, and it hits him. He smiles at Sophia.

                    NICK O′ BRIEN (CONT'D)
          Yeah, Sophia. That sounds great. Wanna walk with me?

Alien tentacles slither out of water fountain right behind them as Nick drapes arm around Sophia, and she holds his draped over hand with a giggle of giddy girly glee, both admiring him and grinning kiddishly to her awestruck, watching classmates as she walks with Nick down hall. They march past Love and her pals, cheerfully. Nick throws surprised Love a haughty look of cocky, merry pride, perhaps to remind her that he goes back onto a very demanding market if she chooses Sammy over him. He raises his eyebrows knowingly at her.

                    SOPHIA KING
          I can help you make her jealous and get back at Sammy
          too.

                    NICK O' BRIEN
               (eyes her, stunned)
          What? I-- I don't-- I wasn't--

                    SOPHIA KING
               (huffs impatiently)
          Don't insult my intelligence, Nick. I know you like Love
          a lot, and you'd love to get back at Sammy for taking her
          away from you. So I'm the perfect person to help you do
          it! And I like you. I've always liked you, Nick. Since 3rd
          grade. So let's have some fun 'n give 'em somethin' to
          talk about.

                    NICK O' BRIEN
               (sheepishly accepts her
               awareness)
          Somethin' like what?

                    SOPHIA KING
          Like this.

Sophia grabs Nick by the collar, pulls him downward towards her and gives him a long kiss on the lips. Love's jaw drops as everyone in the hall stops what they're doing to stare at them. Sophia smiles at dazed, disoriented Nick, who now has red lipstick smeared all over his mouth.

                    SOPHIA KING (CONT'D)
          There, that's better. Oh-- 'n Sammy told me what Uncle
          Romeo and Aunt Juliet said the numbers on our faces
          mean. So if you *really* wanna give him and Love
          something to talk about-- let's you and me maybe talk
          about changin' dem numbers on our faces.

                    NICK O' BRIEN
               (stunned, concerned)

Sophia, Sammy turned 18 this past summer. I turn 18
this spring. Love turns 18 the end of this year. How old
are you again, Sophia?

> SOPHIA KING
> (sighs knowingly)

15.

> NICK O′ BRIEN
> (nods, studying all the zeros all
> over her face)

Yeah, we're not gonna talk about changing *any* of the
numbers on *your* face til you're at *least* 18. You're not
even old enough to *drive* yet, let alone *'fall in love'* 'n get
frisky.

> SOPHIA KING

Am too!

> NICK O'BRIEN

Am not.

> SOPHIA KING

Am too!

> NICK O'BRIEN

Am not.

> SOPHIA KING

Am too!

> NICK O'BRIEN

Am *not*. And I am *not* devirginating my best friend's *15-
year-old* little sister.

> SOPHIA KING

Half-sister.

> NICK O'BRIEN

Still-sister. And infatuation's not the same as deep love,
Sophia. Wait til you get a lil older.

> SOPHIA KING

I don't need to be a *'lil older'*, Nick. I've known you my
whole life. My love is real and my numbers don't lie.

She huffs impatiently and sweeps her shiny bangs out of her face to reveal the #1 on her forehead. Nick is stunned-- Speechless.

                    SOPHIA KING (CONT'D)
          And if you wanna be a gentleman, *fine*. Good for you.
          But if you think Sammy's not gonna try to change the
          numbers on *Love's* face as soon as humanly possible to
          claim her as his 'n only his-- out of *'respect for values'*,
          then--
                    (eyes him skeptically)
          You're not as savvy as I thought.

She steps on her tippy toes, gives a surprised Nick a cute little peck on the cheek, and bounces away down the hall.

                    NICK O′BRIEN
          Just when I thought this couldn't get any weirder-- and
          more complicated...

Nick stares on, displaying a red lip print on his cheek. He glances over at Love, who glares at him in knowing anger as she folds her arms. He shrugs casually at her, trying to gloat and mask discomfort with an awkwardly chill smirk like he's just got it like that, it doesn't phase him.

                    NICK O′BRIEN (CONT'D)
          What?

                    LOVE JONES
          She's a *child*.

                    NICK O′BRIEN
                    (snorting teasingly)
          You're a child.

                    LOVE JONES
          You know what I mean. We're *seniors*. She's like-- a
          bite-sized *freshman*.

                    NICK O′BRIEN
                    (peacocking proudly)
          A bite-sized *sophomore*, who's *madly* in love with her
          big brother's best friend.

                    LOVE JONES
                    (annoyed)
          Yeah. Not cliche at all.

NICK O' BRIEN
What's your point? When we're *married* none of that'll
matter. Though I'll be sure to invite you to the wedding.
Since-- you've already made your choice 'n everything.
In fact, if you're so sure you pick Sammy-- what's it
matter to you *who* I'm with? Unless, of course, it bothers
you because... you're still curiously pondering picking
me...

He grins goofily at her, pleased that he successfully got a rise out of her. She cuts her
eyes at him humorously as she watches him swag on into math class. Then she looks
down with a sobered gulp, in confused and jealous guilt, realizing part of her really does
still want Nick. But she pretends to smile with her chatty, laughing friends, glancing after
Nick sadly. Suddenly Sammy pops up behind Love and gives her a start. She jumps with
a startled giggle and he laughs as she smacks his arm, locking her in a big bear hug and
rocking her side to side, as he kisses her cheek. He gives her the box of chocolates in his
hand as he speaks softly and seductively with a smooth voice to her.

SAMMY KING
Sorry my love's a little late, but it's still sweet 'n
delicious for my delicious sweet. Happy Belated
Valentine's Day, princess.

LOVE JONES
Thank you, Sammy.

She blushes and giggles as he kisses her cheek, handing them to her. Her friends gawk at
him in admiring awe.

KYLE GREEN
Wow, so-- this is-- really happening. You're really here.
It's not, like, a shared delusion or something. K. Jus
gonna have to adjust here.

SAMMY KING
Hey Kyle.

KYLE GREEN
You know my name...

Kyle's stunned. Sammy shrugs.

SAMMY KING
I know all your names. Paula The Cat Lover. Anna The
Fashion Lover. Kyle The Furry Cosplay Lights Lover.
And of course My Love-- My Artistic, Philosophizing,
Melodic Pink Cupcake Lover.

He smiles sweetly at Love. She smiles admiringly at him.

                    LOVE JONES
          I thought *you* were my cupcake?

                    KYLE GREEN
          I'll be your cupcake.

                    SAMMY KING
               (laughs gregariously)
          Hey-- check your crowdfund page. Love told me about
          that procedure you're tryin to get so you can walk again.
          I pinned it to my Insta, Twit 'n Facebook 'n threw a few
          bucks in for you. Should be near your goal by now.

                    KYLE GREEN
               (stunned, eyes wide)
          What-- really? That's a lot of money-- my goal was like
          $10,000...
               (checks phone, gawks)
          Whoa-- I'm at almost 2 million dollars. What did you
          put in? Is this real?

                    SAMMY KING
          Oh I only put in a mill. The other mill musta come from
          everybody else. Looks like you'll finally be walkin,
          dude! Better start sneaker shoppin'. Ya might turn out to
          be a baller. LeBron better watch out!
               (grabs passing jock's basketball
               and dribbles)
          Uh oh. Dude passes ball to Kyle, but a bigger dude
          blocks him. Kyle swivels around, runs like the wind,
          jumps high in the sky like Superman himself 'n SLAM
          DUNKS it into the hoop-- Hooorahh!
               (throws Kyle ball)
          Nothin' but net baby! And the crowd goes wild!
          Screamin' *Kyle! Kyle! Kyle!* Now ya team's got ya on
          their shoulders, cheering you on into the night, and
          every cheerleader knows your name. *Get ready for it.*

Sammy points at laughing Kyle and nods at the girls as Love grins.

                    SAMMY KING (CONT'D)
          Ladies.

                    ANNA KAY
          Hiiiii.

                    PAULA HONEY
          Hi Sammy...

They wave timidly at him with mesmerized slack-jaws.

                    SAMMY KING
          Hey-- I'm throwin a comin' out party on my yacht next
          weekend to celebrate bein' wit my girl Love here. You
          all comin?

                    ANNA KAY
          YEAH! THANKS!

                    PAULA HONEY
          SURE, YEAH!

                    KYLE GREEN
          Why not!

They all chime in simultaneously. Sammy smiles and nods.

                    SAMMY KING
          Aright-- You good?

Sammy looks at Love. She nods with a heart-warmed smile.

                    LOVE JONES
          I'm good.

Sammy kisses her sweetly. His phone rings. He puts a finger up, to gesture that he has to
take this, pointing at his phone. She nods.

                    SAMMY KING
          Deville-- Yeah. I need to see you about somethin'. When
          can we meet?

                    KYLE GREEN
          Man it is *so hard* to *hate* that guy. Like every time I try,
          he jus turns out to be even cooler than he is in TV and
          movies. God, Love. No *wonder* you wanna have his
          babies. *I* wanna have his babies. *And I'm a man!*

The 4 laugh and follow Kyle as he wheels his wheelchair into math class, all while alien
tentacles start slithering out of a nearby locker, towards them, in the emptying school
hall. The tentacles rise high in the air about to strike Love and her friends. But the
tentacles abruptly stop when somebody taps Love on her shoulder. Love turns to see
STABBY SAMMY FAN-- a strange young woman, not as tall as Love, wearing a school

uniform, with mascara running down her cheeks. Love stares at her, stunned and concerned for her.

                         STABBY SAMMY FAN
            Are you Love Jones?

                         LOVE JONES
            Yeah, are-- are you OK?

                         STABBY SAMMY FAN
            You stole Sammy away from us and ruined his life.
            Now you'll pay for ruining mine--

Stabby Sammy Fan suddenly pulls out a butcher knife from behind her back, and raises it high in the air. Love gasps in petrified shock at it as Stabby Sammy Fan quickly lunges it down, toward Love's chest-- and all her nearby classmates scream.

~
See what happens next in Episode 3: "Saving Love"
~

~ *AMAZON.COM GENRE GUIDE* ~

Check out Christi Luv's published works listed below with word count!
If you can't find a title request it at HigherPowerPublishing@Gmail.com

~

~ CURSED ~ FANTASY THRILLERS OF FAITH & HEALING
80K ~ Siren Wars: Hunting Love & The Blood Red Seductress (Novel 1)
30K ~ Princess Wars: Sleeping Beauty & Curse of Pirate Isle (Novella 1)
25K ~ Love Me Tender: The Existence of Sound (Screenplay 1)
10K ~ Survival University: Angel DeVille (Screenplay)
10K ~ Sex, Truth & Videotape: Will Power (Screenplay)
10K ~ Dear Recruiter: 3Shorts~HuntBros/SoulSavrs/HopeHero (Plays)
05K ~ Literary Rants of A 13 Yr. Old Kid: Cyclone's House (Short Story)
TBA ~ Breathe. (Novel)

~

~ TRAPPED ~ BATTLE THRILLERS OF HOPE & ESCAPE
65K ~ The Party: Welcome To Oz (Screenplay 1)
55K ~ Prophet Wars: Mystic Eyes (Screenplay 1)
45K ~ Shadow Wars: Young & Powerful ~ Gin's Escape (Screenplay 1)
30K ~ TP's In His Shoes (Novella)
15K ~ Dear Recruiter: My CRAZY Big Brother! (Novelette)
10K ~ Survival University: Jack In The Box (Screenplay)
10K ~ Sex, Truth & Videotape: The Rumor Mill (Screenplay)
TBA ~ Zombie Wars: *NSYNC SAVES THE WORLD! (Screenplay)

~

~ PUZZLED ~ MYSTERY THRILLERS OF TRUTH & DISCOVERY
160K ~ Killer Secrets of Skyler Stone: My Funny Valentine (Novel 1)
085K ~ TP's The Boy Next Door (Novel)
065K ~ Angel Wars: The Rise of Comet & Lady Phantom (Novel 1)
010K ~ Literary Rants of A 13 Yr Old Kid: Unfinished Business (Play)
010K ~ Survival University: KiLL Club (Novelette)
010K ~ SexTruth&Videotape: Happy Anniversary Dr. Apocalypse (Play)
010K ~ Dear Recruiter: The Superhero-Rape Experiment (Novelette)
*TBA ~ Superhero Wars: The Crossover Games (Novel)

~

~ INVADED ~ ROMANCE THRILLERS OF LOVE & SURVIVAL
250K ~ Virgins vs Aliens: Season1~"Prom King" (13 Screenplay-Novellas)
045K ~ Alien Wars: The Perfect Child (Screenplay 1)
035K ~ Shadow Wars Prequel: Virgins, Vixens & Murder (Audioplay)
010K ~ ST&VT/HottieWars: MrAmerica's CyborgAdventure (Screenplay)
005K ~ Literary Rants: 1 Last Kiss For The Runaway Boy (Short Story)
*TBA ~ TP's Broadway Musicals of Love (Stageplay Series)
*TBA ~ Pop Star Wars: *NSYNC vs BSB ~ Boy Band Battle (Screenplay)
*TBA ~ Supervillains In Love: The Musical (Screenplay)

~

~ AWAKENED ~ NON-FIC INSIGHTS OF LIFE & CONNECTION
10K ~ Dear Recruiter: TDoCL ~ My 1st BF Was A Sociopath (Prose)
10K ~ Sex, Truth & Videotape: TDoCL ~ There's That Hair! (Prose)
10K ~ Survival University: TDoCL ~ iBreathe, Therefore iWrite (Prose)
60K ~ The Diary of Christi Luv: A Love/Life Poetry Collection (Rhyme):

10K ~ The Diary of Christi Luv: Letters in Poetry & Song ~ Dear Youth Life
10K ~ The Diary of Christi Luv: Letters in Poetry & Song ~ Dear Faith Life
10K ~ The Diary of Christi Luv: Letters in Poetry & Song ~ Dear Political Life
10K ~ The Diary of Christi Luv: Letters in Poetry & Song ~ Dear Bad Love
10K ~ The Diary of Christi Luv: Letters in Poetry & Song ~ Dear Puppy Love
10K ~ The Diary of Christi Luv: Letters in Poetry & Song ~ Dear Forever Love
30K ~ The Diary of Christi Luv: Letters in Poetry & Song ~ Dear Life Songs
30K ~ The Diary of Christi Luv: Letters in Poetry & Song ~ Dear Love Songs
~

~ *VIRGINS VS ALIENS ~ S1: "PROM KING" LIST OF EPISODES* ~

**40K ~ Season 01: Episode 01 ~ Wait For Me, My Love*
**20K ~ Season 01: Episode 02 ~ The Virgin Love Triangle*
**20K ~ Season 01: Episode 03 ~ Saving Love*
**20K ~ Season 01: Episode 04 ~ A Love So Selfless*
**20K ~ Season 01: Episode 05 ~ Seduced By Love*
**20K ~ Season 01: Episode 06 ~ Love Seduced By Sammy*
**20K ~ Season 01: Episode 07 ~ The Virgin Love Wedding*
**20K ~ Season 01: Episode 08 ~ Love Seduced By Nick*
**20K ~ Season 01: Episode 09 ~ Virgin Love & War*
**20K ~ Season 01: Episode 10 ~ Virgin Love Secrets*
**25K ~ Season 01: Episode 11 ~ Prom Night Love*
**20K ~ Season 01: Episode 12 ~ Perverting Love*
**30K ~ Season 01: Episode 13 ~ Love's Song*
250K ~ TOTAL COMPLETE S01 ~ "Prom King"
~

~ *COMING SOON* ~

90K ~ MIX: Christi Luv's Mega Collection of Short Stories & Novelettes
55K ~ INVADED: Virgins vs Aliens: S1 "Prom King" ~ Condensed 1/5
50K ~ INVADED: Virgins vs Aliens: S1 "Prom King" ~ Condensed 2/5
45K ~ INVADED: Virgins vs Aliens: S1 "Prom King" ~ Condensed 3/5
50K ~ INVADED: Virgins vs Aliens: S1 "Prom King" ~ Condensed 4/5
40K ~ INVADED: Virgins vs Aliens: S1 "Prom King" ~ Condensed 5/5
TBA ~ MIX: Christi Luv's Mega Collection Series of Long Fiction Samplers
TBA ~ AWAKENED: Luv's Hi5iQ Guide ~ 2Ur Natural Strengths
TBA ~ AWAKENED: Luv's Hi5iQ Guide ~ 2Ur Astro-Angel Strength
TBA ~ AWAKENED: Luv's Hi5iQ Guide ~ 2Ur Secret Strengths
TBA ~ AWAKENED: How 2 Write ~ Hit Songs w/Examples
TBA ~ AWAKENED: How 2 Write ~ Hit Movies w/Examples
TBA ~ AWAKENED: How 2 Write ~ Hit Books w/Examples
*TBA ~ AWAKENED: *HERO Is The New BLACK! ~ Inventors*
*TBA ~ AWAKENED: *HERO Is The New BLACK! ~ Pioneers*
*TBA ~ AWAKENED: *HERO Is The New BLACK! ~ Royalty*
*TBA ~ AWAKENED: *Protecting Our Youth~Kids Rape Kids*
10K ~ AWAKENED: Philosophies Explained ~ Logic of Cursed Books
10K ~ AWAKENED: Philosophies Explained ~ Logic of Trapped Books
10K ~ AWAKENED: Philosophies Explained ~ Logic of Puzzled Books
10K ~ AWAKENED: Philosophies Explained ~ Logic of Invaded Books
10K ~ AWAKENED: Philosophies Explained ~ Logic of Awakened Books
50K ~ AWAKENED: Philosophies Explained ~ Logic of All Luv Books
~

<u>***FULL NON-FICTION TITLES:***</u>

~

**Inspiring Our Youth: HERO Is The New BLACK! ~ A Did You Know? Well You Should!
Collection of Positive Black History Contributions (Word Count TBA)*

**Protecting Our Youth: Kids Rape Kids ~ How To Teach Your Children About Sex Before A
Predator Does (Word Count TBA)*

~

~ *THE 10 COLLECTIONS OF LUV* ~

~

THE ALIEN COLLECTION:
>>>for "Why is this happening to me?" chills & TRUTH fantasy thrills!<<<

~

THE SEDUCTRESS COLLECTION:
>>>for "Is he for real?" chills & ROMANCE fantasy thrills!<<<

~

THE KILLER COLLECTION:
>>>for "Whodunit?" chills & REVENGE fantasy thrills!<<<

~

THE MAD-HATTER COLLECTION:
>>>for "WTF?" chills & ESCAPE fantasy thrills!<<<

~

THE ADVENTURER COLLECTION:
>>>for "What happens next?" chills & ROLLER-COASTER fantasy thrills!<<<

~

THE STUDENT COLLECTION:
>>>for "Will they find out?" chills & VICTORY fantasy thrills!<<<

~

THE ANGEL COLLECTION:
>>>for "How do we fulfill the prophecy?" chills & MAGIC fantasy thrills!<<<

~

THE SUPERHERO COLLECTION:
>>>for "How do we stop the bad guys?" chills & BATTLE fantasy thrills!<<<

~

THE CHARMER COLLECTION:
>>>for "How sweet is that?" chills & FASCINATION fantasy thrills!<<<

~

THE ROCK STAR COLLECTION:
>>>for "When do we rock the stage?" chills & PARTY fantasy thrills!<<<

~

~ *THE ALIEN COLLECTION INCLUDES* ~

Virgins vs Aliens: Complete Season 1 ~ Prom King / E1-13 ~ (250K)
The Diary of Christi Luv: Poetry & Songs ~ All Poems (60K)
Alien Wars: The Perfect Child (45K)
TP's In His Shoes (30K)
Survival University: TDoCL/P.O.A.M: I Breathe, Therefore I Write (10K)
Sex, Truth & Videotape: Hottie Wars ~ A Cyborg Adventure (10K)

~
~ THE SEDUCTRESS COLLECTION INCLUDES ~
Siren Wars: Hunting Love & The Curse of The Blood Red Seductress (80K)
Virgins vs Aliens ~ S1: "Prom King" (Condensed) ~ 1/5 (55K)
Virgins vs Aliens ~ S1: "Prom King" (Condensed) ~ 2/5 (50K)
Virgins vs Aliens ~ S1: "Prom King" (Condensed) ~ 3/5 (45K)
Virgins vs Aliens ~ S1: "Prom King" (Condensed) ~ 4/5 (50K)
Virgins vs Aliens ~ S1: "Prom King" (Condensed) ~ 5/5 (40K)
Sex, Truth & Videotape: The Full Shorts & Novelettes Collection (35K)
Sex, Truth & Videotape: Will Power (10K)
The Diary of Christi Luv: Poetry & Songs ~ Bad Love (10K)
Sex, Truth & Videotape: TDoCL/POA Memoir ~ There's That Hair! (10K)

~
~ THE KILLER COLLECTION INCLUDES ~
The Killer Secrets of Skyler Stone: My Funny Valentine (160K)
TP's The Boy Next Door (85K)
Survival University: KiLL Club (10K)
Literary Rants of A 13 Year Old Kid: Cyclone's House (5K)
Protecting Our Youth: Kids Rape Kids (TBA)

~
~ THE MAD-HATTER COLLECTION INCLUDES ~
The Party: Welcome To Oz (65K)
Dear Recruiter: The Full Shorts & Novelettes Collection (30K)
Dear Recruiter: My CRAZY Big Brother! (15K)
Dear Recruiter: TDoCL/P.O.A.M. ~ My 1st BF Was A Sociopath (10K)
The Diary of Christi Luv: Poetry & Songs ~ Political Life (10K)
Sex, Truth & Videotape: Happy Anniversary, Dr. Apocalypse! (10K)

~
~ THE ADVENTURER COLLECTION INCLUDES ~
Luv's Mega Collection of Short Stories & Novelettes (90K)
Princess Wars: Sleeping Beauty & The Curse of Pirate Island (30K)
The Diary of Christi Luv: Poetry & Songs ~ Forever Love (10K)
Literary Rants of A 13 Yr Old Kid: 1 Last Kiss For The Runaway Boy (5K)
Cursed/Trapped/Puzzled/Invaded/Awakened Genre Samplers (TBA)

~
~ THE STUDENT COLLECTION INCLUDES ~
Prophet Wars: Mystic Eyes (55K)
Survival University: The Full Shorts & Novelettes Collection (40K)
The Diary of Christi Luv: Poetry & Songs ~ Youth Life (10K)
Survival University: Jack In The Box (10K)
Sex, Truth & Videotape: The Rumor Mill (10K)
How 2 Write: Hit Movies w/Examples (TBA)
How 2 Write: Hit Books w/Examples (TBA)

~
~ THE ANGEL COLLECTION INCLUDES ~
Angel Wars: The Rise of Comet & Lady Phantom (65K)
Survival University: Angel DeVille (10K)
The Diary of Christi Luv: Poetry & Songs ~ Faith Life (10K)
Literary Rants of A 13 Year Old Kid: Unfinished Business (10K)
Breathe. (TBA)

Luv's Hi5iQ Guide: 2Ur Astro-Angel Strengths (TBA)
Luv's Hi5iQ Guide: 2Ur Natural Strengths (TBA)
Luv's Hi5iQ Guide: 2Ur Secret Strengths (TBA)

~

~ *THE SUPERHERO COLLECTION INCLUDES* ~

Shadow Wars: The Young & The Powerful ~ Gin's Escape (45K)
The Diary of Christi Luv: Poetry & Songs ~ Life Songs (30K)
Dear Recruiter: The Superhero-Rape Experiment (10K)
Survival University: 3 Shorts ~ Hunt Bros / Soul Savers / Hope Heroes (10K)
Zombie Wars: *NSYNC SAVES THE WORLD! (TBA)
Superhero Wars: The Crossover Games (TBA)
HERO Is The New BLACK! ~ Inventors (TBA)
HERO Is The New BLACK! ~ Pioneers (TBA)
HERO Is The New BLACK! ~ Royalty (TBA)

~

~ *THE CHARMER COLLECTION INCLUDES* ~

Luv's Mega Collection of Long Fiction Samplers (165K)
Philosophies Explained: The Logic of All Luv Books (55K)
Love Me Tender: The Existence of Sound (25K)
Literary Rants of A 13 Year Old Kid: Total Collection (25K)
The Diary of Christi Luv: Poetry & Songs ~ Puppy Love (10K)
Philosophies Explained: The Logic of Cursed Books (10K)
Philosophies Explained: The Logic of Trapped Books (10K)
Philosophies Explained: The Logic of Puzzled Books (10K)
Philosophies Explained: The Logic of Invaded Books (10K)
Philosophies Explained: The Logic of Awakened Books (10K)

~

~ *THE ROCK STAR COLLECTION INCLUDES* ~

The Young & Powerful/SW Prequel ~ Real Talk: Virgins, Vixens & Murder (35K)
The Diary of Christi Luv: Poetry & Songs ~ Love Songs (10K)
Pop Star Wars: *NSYNC vs BSB ~ Battle of The Boy Bands (TBA)
TP's 4 Broadway Musicals of Love Series (TBA)
Supervillains In Love: The Musical (TBA)
How 2 Write: Hit Songs w/Examples (TBA)

~

~ *STAY UPDATED* ~

Follow The Author @ amazon.com/author/christiluv
Subscribe 4 Freebies @ christiluvtv.wix.com/VIPclub
Order A Book Subscription @ Patreon.com/AmazonBookClub
Donate To Author Projects @ Patreon.com/ChristiLuvTV
Tip The Author Just Because @ PayPal.com/ChristiLuvTV
or Venmo.com/ChristiLuvTV
or make it easiest @ TinyURL.com/SquareMonthly

~

Thank you for purchasing this book. Hope you enjoyed the journey!
God Bless-- and see you soon, on the next one!

~

~ *ADULT MATURITY GUIDE* ~

TBD = To Be Determined
MHI = Mentioned, Hinted or Implied
Most Language = YA-safe {PG-13}
LPG = Language MG-appropriate {PG}

KISS = MG-(Mid-Grade/Kid)-Safe Hetero Affection (Crush's Sweet Peck)
TOUCH = YA-(Young-Adult/Teen)-OK Hetero Affection (Like Making Out)
SEX = NA-(New-Adult/AFTER-High-School)-Restricted Hetero Affection
(Sodomy / deviant sex is rarely implied or depicted & not encouraged)
RAPE = Sexual Violence / Spiritually Intimate Robbery

NRV = Non-sexual "Real" (Reality) Violence
NFV = Non-sexual "Fake" (Fantasy) Violence
DRINK = Recreational Use of Alcohol
DRUG = Recreational Use of Nicotine or Narcotics

BOOK:::::: KISS/TOUCH ~ SEX-/-RAPE ~ NRV/NFV ~ DRINK/DRUG

3ShortStories: No/No ~~~~ No/Yes ~~~~ Yes/Yes ~~~~~~MHI/No
**Alien Wars 1:* Yes/Yes ~~ Marital/Repro ~ Yes/Yes ~~~~~ Mom/No
Angel DeVille: Yes/No ~~~~ MHI/No ~~~~ Meh/Yes ~~~~~MHI/No
Angel Wars 1: Yes/No ~~~~ No/No ~~~~~ No/Yes ~~~ No/No/LPG
DearRecruiter: No/No ~~~~ MHI/Yes ~~~~Yes/Yes ~~~~~ No/No
DrApocalypse: Yes/Yes ~~ Marital/No ~~~No/No ~~~~~~No/No
***Hottie Wars:* No/No ~~~~ MHI/No ~~~~ No/Yes ~~~~~~No/No
****Jack In Box:* No/No ~~~~ No/No ~~~~~ No/No ~~~~~ MHI/No
******KiLL Club:* No/No ~~~~ MHI/Yes ~~~~Yes/No ~~~~~~ No/No
**Lit Rants/Kid:* Yes/No ~~~~No/No ~~~~ Yes/Yes ~~~~ No/No/LPG
LoveMeTendr: Yes/Yes ~~~~No/No ~~~~ Yes/Meh ~~~~ Once/No
PrincessWar1: Yes/Yes ~~~~No/No ~~~~ Yes/Yes ~~~~ Pirates/No
ProphetWars1: Yes/No ~~~~No/No ~~~~ No/Yes ~~~~ No/No/LPG
SexTruthVido: Yes/Yes ~ Marital/Attempt ~ Yes/Yes ~~~~~~ No/No
ShadowWars1: Yes/Yes ~~ Yes/Attempt ~~ Yes/No ~~~~~~ No/No
SH-R Exprimnt: No/MHI ~~~ No/MHI ~~~~ MHI/No ~~~~~~ No/No
**Siren Wars 1:* Yes/Yes ~~ MHI/Attempt ~~ Yes/Yes ~~~~~~ No/No
SkylerStone 1: Yes/Yes ~~~ MHI/Yes ~~~~ Yes/No ~~~No/Rejected
SurvivalUnivrs: No/No ~~~~ MHI/Yes ~~~ Yes/Yes ~~~~~~~MHI/No
***Y&P Prequel:* Yes/Yes ~~~~Yes/No ~~~ Yes/No ~~~~~~ Yes/No
The Party / Oz: Yes/Yes ~~~~MHI/No ~~~ Meh/Yes ~~~No/PopField
The RumorMill: No/No ~~~ No/Attempt ~~ Yes/No ~~~~~~No/No
TPsInHisShoes: No/No ~~~~~No/No ~~~~Yes/No~~~~~~ MHI/No
TPsBoyNxDoor: Yes/No ~~~~ No/No ~~~~ Yes/No ~~~Stepdad/No
VirginsVsAlien: Yes/Yes ~~ MHI/Attempt ~~ Yes/Yes ~~~~~ Yes/No
*****Will Power:* Yes/Meh ~~~ MHI/No ~~~~ No/No ~~~~~~ No/No

~ *ORDER OF BOOKS BY YEAR OF COPYRIGHT* ~

Most concepts/titles are not listed because they are not yet in development.
Entire Title May Not Be Spelled Out But Represents Series Franchise

~ *1990's* ~

1990's COPYRIGHT OF COMPLETED SHORT & FULL LENGTH SCRIPTS

MOST NEW CONCEPTS/TITLES: Original = 1997-2002 / 1st Published = 2017
LITERARY RANTS/13YRKID: 1st Scripts = 1997 / 1st Published/Proofed = 2020
***********HUNTING LOVE: Idea/Title = 1997 / 1st Published/Updated = 2017
*************WILL POWER: Idea/Title = 1998 / 1st Published/Updated = 2020
***POEM/SONG~SAMPLER: Original = 1999 / 1st Published/Updated = 2019
POEM/SONG~COLLECTION: Original = 1999 / 1st Published/Updated = 2020
*POEM/SONG~YOUTH LIFE: Original = 1999 / 1st Published/Updated = 2020
**POEM/SONG~FAITH LIFE: Original = 1999 / 1st Published/Updated = 2020
POEM/SONG~POLITIC LIFE: Original = 1999 / 1st Published/Updated = 2020
**POEM/SONG~BAD LOVE: Original = 1999 / 1st Published/Updated = 2020
POEM/SONG~PUPPY LOVE: Original = 1999 / 1st Published/Updated = 2020
POEM/SONG~FOREVER <3: Original = 1999 / 1st Published/Updated = 2020
*POEM/SONG~LIFE SONGS: Original = 1999 / 1st Published/Updated = 2020
POEM/SONG~LOVE SONGS: Original = 1999 / 1st Published/Updated = 2020

~ *2000's* ~

2000's COPYRIGHT OF COMPLETED SHORT & FULL LENGTH SCRIPTS

MANY NEW CONCEPTS/TITLES: Original = 2002-2010 / 1st Published = 2020
PROM KING (Virgins vs Aliens basis): Movie Script = 2000 / 1st Pub = 2020
BITE ME: My Valley-Girl-Wolf Idea = 2005 / TP's Valley-Boy Spin/Play = 2008
************JACK IN THE BOX: 1st Script = 2005 / 1st Published = 2020
ALIEN WARS/PERFECT CHILD: Idea/Title = 2005 / 1st Published = 2017
*****COMET/LADY PHANTOM: Idea/Title = 2007 / 1st Published = 2017
**************ANGEL WARS: 1st Script = 2008 / 1st Published = 2017
**TP'S THE BOY NEXT DOOR: 1st Script = 2009 / 1st Published = 2020

~ *2010's* ~

2010's COPYRIGHT OF COMPLETED SHORT & FULL LENGTH SCRIPTS

SOME NEW CONCEPTS/TITLES: Original = 2013-2017 / 1st Published = 2017
*****PROPHET WARS: Concept/Title = 2010 / 1st Published/Updated = 2020
*****PRINCESS WARS: Concept/Title = 2010 / 1st Published/Updated = 2017
*********SIREN WARS: Concept/Title = 2010 / 1st Published/Updated = 2017
***************ANGEL DEVILLE: 1st Script = 2013 / 1st Published = 2020
********THE HUNT BROTHERS: 1st Script = 2013 / 1st Published = 2020
***********THE SOUL SAVERS: 1st Script = 2013 / 1st Published = 2020
********HAPPY HOPE HEROES: 1st Script = 2013 / 1st Published = 2020
************THE RUMOR MILL: 1st Script = 2013 / 1st Published = 2020
******************KiLL CLUB: 1st Script = 2013 / 1st Published = 2020
********YOUNG & POWERFUL: 1st Script = 2013 / 1st Published = 2020

***********LOVE ME TENDER: 1st Script = 2015 / 1st Published = 2020
ALIEN WARS/PERFECT CHILD: 1st Script = 2015 / 1st Published = 2017
*SECRETS OF SKYLER STONE: 1st Script = 2015 / 1st Published = 2017
************PROPHET WARS: 1st Script = 2015 / 1st Published = 2020
***************SIREN WARS: 1st Script = 2017 / 1st Published = 2017
***************ANGEL WARS: Updated = 2017 / 1st Published = 2017
************PRINCESS WARS: 1st Script = 2017 / 1st Published = 2017
*************HOTTIE WARS: 1st Script = 2017 / 1st Published = 2017
**********TP's IN HIS SHOES: 1st Script = 2017 / 1st Published = 2020
VIRGINS vs ALIENS (Prom King Update): New Scripts = 2018 / 1st Pub= 2020
****************THE PARTY: 1st Script = 2018 / 1st Published = 2019
*SHADOW WARS/GIN STORY: 1st Script = 2019 / 1st Published = 2020
**DEAR RECRUITER: 1st Poem/Idea/Title = 2019 / 1st Published = 2020

~ *2020's* ~

2020's COPYRIGHT OF COMPLETED SHORT & FULL LENGTH SCRIPTS

*A FEW NEW CONCEPT/TITLES: Original = 2017-Now / 1st Published = 2020
******************WILL POWER: 1st Script = 2020 / 1st Published = 2020
HAPPY ANVRSY DR APOCALYPSE: 1st Script = 2020 / 1st Published = 2020
**MY 1ST BF WAS A SOCIOPATH: 1st Script = 2020 / 1st Published = 2020
**iBREATHE THEREFORE iWRITE: 1st Script = 2020 / 1st Published = 2020
*******MY CRAZY BIG BROTHER: 1st Script = 2020 / 1st Published = 2020
SUPERHERO-RAPE EXPERIMENT: 1st Script = 2020 / 1st Published = 2020
*********SURVIVAL UNIVERSITY: 1st Series = 2020 / 1st Published = 2020
*****SEX, TRUTH & VIDEOTAPE: 1st Series = 2020 / 1st Published = 2020

COPYRIGHT OF CONCEPTS & TITLES NOW IN DEVELOPMENT

***SUPERHERO WARS: Concept/Title = 2010 / 1st Published Script = 2020
******MONSTER WARS: Concept/Title = 2010 / 1st Published Script = 2020
*******ZOMBIE WARS: Concept/Title = 2010 / 1st Published Script = 2020
***********BREATHE.: Concept/Title = 2010 / 1st Published Script = 2020
***LUV HI5IQ GUIDES: Concept/Title = 2015 / 1st Published Script = 2020
***LUV HOW 2 WRITE: Concept/Title = 2015 / 1st Published Script = 2020
*HERO IS NEW BLACK: Concept/Title = 2015 / 1st Published Script = 2020
PROTECT OUR YOUTH: Concept/Title = 2015 / 1st Published Script = 2020
*****POP STAR WARS: Concept/Title = 2018 / 1st Published Script = 2020
****ROCK STAR WARS: Concept/Title = 2018 / 1st Published Script = 2020
*******NSYNC VS BSB: Concept/Title = 2018 / 1st Published Script = 2020
*TP'S LOVE MUSICALS: Concept/Title = 2018 / 1st Published Script = 2020
**LUV MEGA SAMPLES: Concept/Title = 2018 / 1st Published Script = 2020
*LUV GENRE SAMPLES: Concept/Title = 2018 / 1st Published Script = 2020
SUPERVILLAINSinLOVE: Concept/Title = 2019 / 1st Published Script = 2020
******KIDS RAPE KIDS: Concept/Title = 2020 / 1st Published Script = 2020
PHILOSOPHY EXPLAIN: Concept/Title = 2020 / 1st Published Script = 2020
WHAT ACTOR R YOU?: Concept/Title = 2020 / 1st Published Script = 2020
NSYNC SAVES WORLD: Concept/Title = 2020 / 1st Published Script = 2020

List will be updated over time as more titles/scripts are completed!

~ *AMAZON.COM TIME & WORD COUNT GUIDE* ~

To Christi Luv's Published & Partner Works ~ Count subject to change
TDoCL = The Diary of Christi Luv / POC = Proof of Concept

NOVELS & MOVIE-LENGTH PLAYS (WORKS OVER 40K WORDS & PRESUMABLY OVER 90 MINUTES IN ADAPTED SCREEN TIME):
165K ~ Luv's Mega Collection of Long Fiction Samplers (Prose & Plays)
160K ~ The Killer Secrets of Skyler Stone: My Funny Valentine (Prose)
120K ~ TP's Mega Collection of Long Fiction Samplers (Prose & Plays)
*90K ~ Luv's Mega Collection of Short Stories & Novelettes (P&P)
*85K ~ TP's The Boy Next Door (Prose)
*80K ~ Siren Wars: Hunting Love / Blood Red Seductress Curse (Prose)
*65K ~ The Party: Welcome To Oz (Screenplay)
*65K ~ Angel Wars: The Rise of Comet & Lady Phantom (Prose)
*60K ~ Philosophies Explained: The Logic of All Christi Luv Books (Mix)
*60K ~ The Diary of Christi Luv: Poetry & Song ~ All Poems (Rhyme)
*55K ~ Prophet Wars: Mystic Eyes (Screenplay)
*55K ~ Virgins vs Aliens: Prom King ~ Condensed (Screenplays) 1/5
*50K ~ Virgins vs Aliens: Prom King ~ Condensed (Screenplays) 2/5
*50K ~ Virgins vs Aliens: Prom King ~ Condensed (Screenplays) 4/5
*45K ~ Shadow Wars: Young & Powerful ~ Gin's Escape (Screenplay)
*45K ~ Virgins vs Aliens: Prom King ~ Condensed (Screenplays) 3/5
*45K ~ Alien Wars: The Perfect Child (Screenplay)
*40K ~ Virgins vs Aliens: Prom King ~ Condensed (Screenplays) 5/5

NOVELLAS & TV-LENGTH PLAYS (WORKS 17K – 40K WORDS & PRESUMABLY 60 TO 90 MINUTES IN ADAPTED SCREEN TIME):
250K ~ Virgins vs Aliens: S1 ~ "Prom King" (13 Screenplay-Novellas)
*40K ~ Survival University: Shorts & Novelettes (Screenplays & Prose)
*35K ~ Young & Powerful Prequel: Virgins, Vixens & Murder (Audioplay)
*35K ~ Sex, Truth & Videotape: Shorts & Novelettes (Plays & Prose)
*30K ~ Princess Wars: Sleeping Beauty & Curse of Pirate Isle (Prose)
*30K ~ Dear Recruiter: Spykult Shorts & Novelettes (All Prose)
*30K ~ TP's In His Shoes (Prose)
*30K ~ The Diary of Christi Luv: Poetry & Song ~ Life Songs (Rhyme)
*30K ~ The Diary of Christi Luv: Poetry & Song ~ Love Songs (Rhyme)
*25K ~ Love Me Tender: The Existence of Sound (Screenplay)
*20K ~ Literary Rants of A 13 Yr. Old Kid: Shorts & Flash-Fiction (Prose)

NOVELETTES & SHORT-FILM POC PLAYS (7K ☐ 17K WORDS & PRESUMABLY 30 TO 60 MINUTES IN ADAPTED SCREEN TIME):
*15K ~ DEAR RECRUITER: My CRAZY Big Brother! (Prose)
*10K ~ DEAR RECRUITER: The Superhero-Rape Experiment (Prose)
*10K ~ DEAR RECRUITER: TDOCL ~ My 1st BF Was A Sociopath (Prose)
*10K ~ DEAR RECRUITER: 3 Shorts (Stage & Screenplays)

*10K ~ SURVIVAL UNIVERSITY: Angel DeVille (Screenplay)
*10K ~ SURVIVAL UNIVERSITY: TDoCL/iBreathe Therefore iWrite (Prose)
*10K ~ SURVIVAL UNIVERSITY: KiLL Club (Prose)
*10K ~ SURVIVAL UNIVERSITY: Jack In The Box (Screenplay)
*10K ~ SEX, TRUTH & VIDEOTAPE: TDoCL ~ There's That Hair! (Prose)
*10K ~ SEX, TRUTH & VIDEOTAPE: Dr. Apocalypse! (Screenplay)
*10K ~ SEX, TRUTH & VIDEOTAPE: Will Power (Screenplay)
*10K ~ SEX, TRUTH & VIDEOTAPE: The Rumor Mill (Screenplay)
*10K ~ SEX, T&V: Hottie Wars~ Mr. America's Cyborg Adventure (Play)
*10K ~ LITERARY RANTS EPISODE: Unfinished Business (Prose)
*10K ~ PHILOSOPHIES EXPLAINED: Logic of Luv's Cursed Books (Mix)
*10K ~ PHILOSOPHIES EXPLAINED: Logic of Luv's Trapped Books (Mix)
*10K ~ PHILOSOPHIES EXPLAINED: Logic of Luv's Puzzled Books (Mix)
*10K ~ PHILOSOPHIES EXPLAINED: Logic of Luv's Invaded Books (Mix)
*10K ~ PHILOSOPHIES EXPLAINED: Logic of Luv's Awakened Books (Mx)
*10K ~ THE DIARY OF CHRISTI LUV: Poetry&Song/Political Life (Rhyme)
*10K ~ THE DIARY OF CHRISTI LUV: Poetry&Song/Faith Life (Rhyme)
*10K ~ THE DIARY OF CHRISTI LUV: Poetry&Song/Youth Life (Rhyme)
*10K ~ THE DIARY OF CHRISTI LUV: Poetry&Song/Puppy Love (Rhyme)
*10K ~ THE DIARY OF CHRISTI LUV: Poetry&Song/Bad Love (Rhyme)
*10K ~ THE DIARY OF CHRISTI LUV: Poetry&Song/ForeverLove (Rhyme)

***SHORT STORIES & SKIT-LENGTH POC PLAYS (1K☐7K WORDS &
PRESUMABLY 5 TO 30 MINUTES IN ADAPTED SCREEN TIME):***
***5K ~ 3 SHORTS: The Hunt Brothers (Screenplay)
***5K ~ 3 SHORTS: The Soul Savers (Screenplay)
***5K ~ 3 SHORTS: The Happy Hope Heroes (Stageplay)
***5K ~ LITERARY RANTS EPISODE: 1 Last Kiss For The Runaway Boy
***5K ~ LITERARY RANTS EPISODE: Cyclone's House

***FLASH FICTION & AD-LENGTH POC PLAYS (UNDER 1K WRDS &
PRESUMABLY UNDER 5 MINUTES IN ADAPTED SCREEN TIME):***
*TBA ~ Literary Rants of A 13 Year-old Kid: Various Unlisted Segments

IN PROGRESS...
*TBA ~ Breathe. (Novel)
*TBA ~ Superhero Wars: The Crossover Games (Novel)
*TBA ~ Zombie Wars: *NSYNC SAVES THE WORLD! (Screenplay)
*TBA ~ Pop Star Wars: NSYNC vs BSB ~ Boy Band Battle (Screenplay)
*TBA ~ Supervillains In Love: The Musical (Screenplay)
*TBA ~ TP's Broadway Musicals of Love (Stageplay Series)

AD-LENGTH = Quick TV Commercial Length
SKIT-LENGTH = Long Sneak Preview Length
POC = Proof of Concept